PECCANT

PECCANT

The Beginning

B. L. BRYANT

authorHOUSE®

AuthorHouse™ LLC
1663 Liberty Drive
Bloomington, IN 47403
www.authorhouse.com
Phone: 1-800-839-8640

Published by AuthorHouse   08/18/2014

ISBN: 978-1-4969-2814-6 (sc)
ISBN: 978-1-4969-2813-9 (e)

Library of Congress Control Number: 2014913293

CHAPTER 1

It was a beautiful hot June morning as she began to throw her clothes into her suitcases, excited for what the trip was going to bring her! She had made up her mind, she was going to do something different this summer. She was going to do something wild and impetuous. Her life had always been predictable and she was ready for change! With the suitcases heavy in her hands she smiled as her ride pulled into the driveway. She turned to say goodbye to her family as she jumped into the van. Being only 18 years old she was wise for her years. Like any other teenager she wasn't sure what she wanted out of life, but knew she was wanting to make a difference. Very smart, but a big dreamer. Her name was Bridget, born during a difficult Southern Indiana winter in 1982. The family she was born into was considered poor, but that didn't kill her spirit. Being poor made her stronger and kinder. Her family weren't beggers, they worked hard for everything they had. Bridget had an amazingly big heart. All she ever wanted to do was help others in any way that she could. She had an older brother named Greg and a younger sister named Sophia. Bridget's mom stayed at home to raise the kids while her dad worked all day to try to earn money for his family. Although losing his job at times due to layoffs, her father still was a kind hearted man. Often times Bridget felt invisible to the family. She went through life wanting to be something, to make her parents proud. But, graduating from high school was rough. Her grades weren't all that great on the account of her daydreaming and not paying attention to her studies. During her Junior and Senior years in school she met a boy named Jon Spencer. An athletic type of a boy, with dark brown hair and brown eyes. Not a very tall man, he stood 5 foot 9 inches with a slight muscular build. He had a passion for boxing and Bridget would enjoy his boxing matches after school. Jon was the class clown of the school so he didn't have to worry much about any fighting. His dream was to move to Hollywood to attend acting school and become an actor. Bridget was impressed with his dreams, but never intended to follow him to where he was going. Being an average looking girl with blonde hair and blue eyes she knew she was no Angelina Jolie. She stood 5 foot 4 inches with a petite build. Bridget had a natural beauty look to her, but not enough to be considered a model in her eyes. After graduation Jon, Bridget and her two best friends Beverly and Tina were planning a summer trip to Canada. Beverly was a bit taller than Bridget with dark blonde hair and green eyes with a slender build. Tina was shorter a mere 5 foot 2 inches tall with dark hair and blue eyes. Her frame was a little bigger than Bridget's, but very cute all the same. This would be their last hoorah before they all went to college or found jobs to become the usual boring adult. Beverly had plans to attend dental school and Tina, along with Bridget, didn't know what she wanted to pursue in life. Bridget knew on this trip she and Jon wouldn't be a couple any longer. Jon wanted to keep the relationship going but, Bridget never intended on giving her heart to him. She knew what his dreams were. She feared that if she fell in love with Jon, her heart would be broken if he fell for one of the beautiful actress' he would star in any movie with. This was Bridget though. She was always level headed and knew how to protect herself. Although she did care deeply for Jon, she knew it wouldn't work out in the long run. They agreed to always be friends no matter what happened in their lives and he would always be a rock for her to depend on. Later in life she should figure out just how important Jon would be in her life. That June, after graduation the road trip was on! They were all excited as they set out on the open road heading north out of Salem, Indiana. The trip was going to be very long but, very much worth it. After arriving in Canada they found the summer house they were going to be renting for the next two and a half months. Everyone was bubbling over with excitement as they ran into the house with all their stuff in tow. Tina piped up, "This is going to be an amazing summer!" Beverly jokingly prodded at Tina's sides, "Sure, as long as you don't get drunk every time we turn around." Bridget came walking in the front door with a huge bag thrown over her shoulder. "This house seems pretty nice to spend the summer in. I expected it to be a bit smaller. So what does everyone want to do?" She asked staring at the two tired girls. "Bridget, I would like to just pass out the trip made me a bit sleepy," Jon said as he flopped down on the couch to take a quick nap. Everyone agreed it would be best to just rest up for the next day or two before doing anything special. That Thursday was the day Bridget's life would change forever. She, Tina, and Beverly headed down the street to a small café to grab something to eat. Jon wanted to stay behind to finish up his college preparation list. The girls sat down at a table a few feet from the front door and began to talk about silly things. "Bridget, why don't you show us the latest Saturday Night Live skit you seen last week it is so hilarious," Tina giggled. Bridget enjoyed being a jokester herself, but being silly in public made her nervous. She thought for a moment and shouted, "Are you crazy Tina I am not doing that in public!" "You are such a chicken!" Beverly challenged rolling her eyes. One thing about Bridget was she had a great sense of humor and also a very competitive side. "Okay fine I accept that silly challenge to prove I am not a chicken." Bridget said standing up and began to portray her version of the recent skit. Little did she know coming in the door behind her were seven very well dressed people. A mix of guys and girls came in to relax after their hard afternoon. Three of the crowd had gotten past Bridget while she danced around with her back to them. Just as she spun around swinging her arm violently a handsome man came in the door directly behind her. Before she knew it her hand smacked him very hard across the face. "Oh my god, I am so sorry I didn't see you there!" Bridget gasped covering her mouth in embarrassment. He stood staring into her eyes for a few seconds while she felt a little hypnotized by his gaze. She quickly made her way to her seat as Tina and Beverly continued to laugh under their breath. The rest of the crowd went ahead and sat down, while the man who Bridget smacked turned around to give her another quick look without saying a word. He seemed confused while he kept looking up from his table to glance at her. Bridget noticed how handsome he was, but she also noticed the beauty sitting right next to him. She had long dark wavy hair, big blue eyes and a figure most women would kill for. She also looked as though she should star in a porno Bridget thought as she giggled to herself. The man she hit had intense brown eyes, short blonde hair and a slight muscular build almost identical to Jon's. The girls sat at their table for a few more minutes and then decided it would be best if they left. Bridget was feeling extremely foolish and didn't feel the need to prolong her anguish. As they left the café nobody bothered to look back at the crowd that came in. The crowd seemed to be having a good laugh at the girls' expense. When the girls returned home Beverly and Tina explained what had happened to Jon. Bridget sheepishly said, "Alright guys that is enough I am embarrassed the way it is and it is all your fault! You challenged me." Tina and Beverly continued to laugh it off as Jon stood up to get his drink. "Bridget, you are always putting yourself in these situations. First, it's a shame I missed it and second I will miss your clumsy ass when I move away." Bridget smirked, "Ha, Ha very funny Jon." Tina spoke up to give her input on the crowd they seen at the café, "I think every single guy that came strolling in there would look good posing in a beefcake calendar." All three girls started laughing hysterically while Jon rolled his eyes, "I have to go take a shower and I think it would be a good idea if you do the same, Tina." Later that night everyone decided to head to a club in town that allowed eighteen year olds to enjoy dancing without the added enjoyment of alcohol. Bridget vowed she would not make a fool of herself this night and she knew she would stick to that. She never slow danced out of fear of stepping on tender toes. As everyone sat down Beverly looked up with a gaping mouth. As soon as Tina started to ask what her problem was, the man from the café came walking up to the table. "Hello, I thought I would come over and introduce myself. My name is James Mackenvoy." Bridget sat with her mouth open as well without saying a word. James held out his hand to shake theirs. When he offered his hand out to shake Bridget's he said, "You know the guy you smacked across the face?" When he started to smile at her Bridget felt more at ease. "Hi, my name is Bridget Case and I am so sorry about that really I did not see you." "It's ok," James said as he stepped back a bit. "I realized it was a mistake on your part, but a funny one at that. I am not unaccustomed to being hit from time to time. Would you mind if we join you?" James asked as he motioned for everyone to come over. Jon was about to say no, but everyone was already starting over to the table. He had an uneasy feeling about James from the start. Something told him he was bad news. When everyone walked over James began to introduce everyone. "I will start with my friend here Jackie Cook, this is my brother Marcus Mackenvoy, his girl Olivia, my cousin Cullen Mackenvoy, my best friend Matt Williams and his girl Cindy." Everyone smiled as they kindly said hello. Marcus had short dark hair and dark eyes like his brother with the same build. Olivia wasn't a knockout, but a natural beauty with long brown hair and green eyes. Cullen was very handsome. He was tall with a muscular build and dark wavy hair that flowed around his ears and down around the back of his neck. He also had the same dark eyes as his cousins. Matt had short brown hair with blue eyes with a tall build. Cindy had short strawberry blonde hair with dark brown eyes. Bridget introduced everyone at her table and when Jon reached out to shake James' hand he gave him a simple nod. James could tell Jon wasn't too happy with him joining the table. They all talked for hours learning each other's personalities. Jackie was like Jon in the fact that she wasn't too happy with the whole situation. Her dismay was for other reasons. She felt as though everyone in her crowd were above Bridget and her friends. But, she was very intrigued with Jon. Of course, Jon did have that charm about himself. That was one of the reasons Bridget shied away from giving him her heart. Bridget couldn't help but notice James' eyes continually looking at her face. It wasn't like he was ogling her in a rude way. There was something about the way he was looking at her that was making her heart skip a beat. Cullen was a funny sort of guy like Jon. Looking at him you would think he would be a bully, but he was very pleasant to be around. Later, Bridget would find out how powerful and cunning Cullen really was. Marcus along with Olivia had a reserved personality, but very kind. Matt and James were obviously best friends, they complimented each other quiet well with the joking back and forth. A very interesting fact about James and his crowd came to surface during their chat. "Well, I guess I should let you all know, all of us guys sitting here will be famous one day," James said as he took a big gulp of his drink. "Oh yeah, you don't say? Me as well," Jon said. Cullen looked at Jon quickly and asked, "No kidding? What will be your claim to fame?" "I will be off to acting school in Hollywood California soon." Jon said with pride. "That is amazing!" Cindy said smiling at Jon. "Now, what about you guys?" Jon asked. James looked at the guys and smiled, "We have our own alternative rock band. Cullen here is the drummer, I am the lead and vocals, Matt here is the vocals and rhythm, and my brother is the bass guitarist. If you ever want to come hear us play we have been renting this theater to practice in." James smiled as he invited them along. "Well, we have a lot going on..." Jon started to say, but was interrupted by Tina, "Yes! I love music like that! What stuff do you play?" Matt said, "We like to play stuff like Alice in Chains, Metallica, Ac-Dc that sort of thing." "They are really fantastic." Olivia said with pride as she rubbed Marcus' arm. Jackie continued to watch James eye Bridget and she began to feel a bit angry so she stood up and said, "I think we all better be going I am getting a little tired." James and the guys all stood up thanking Bridget and her friends for a nice evening, but he didn't leave without letting her know they would all see each other again soon. On the days the band had practices Tina and Beverly couldn't get Bridget to go watch them play. Jon wasn't exactly thrilled with seeing them play and she felt a little weird inside when James was around. During their little meet ups at the club she was really starting to enjoy listening to him talk and especially watching him move. She couldn't help to feel guilty with Jon sitting there as well. She knew he could sense the tension. Not to mention Jackie who obviously did not like Bridget. Nobody in Bridget's crowd really knew anything about these Mackenvoys. She was curious and wanted to know more, but what was the point really? She knew after summer she would never see them again. She did find out they were all from Southern Tennessee in a small town called Pleasantville. It sounded very nice. These people were some of the best people she had ever met, or so she thought. After a couple of weeks of begging, Tina talked Bridget into going to watch the band play. She hid behind the entry way door to listen and Olivia was right. These guys were amazing! They did have a similar sound to Alice in Chains. James' voice was very sexy and deep when he would sing while Matt had a higher type of voice. Bridget stared in amazement. Watching how James' fingers slid down the neck of the guitar. She found herself feeling sexually excited. She felt her face feeling flushed. Then all the sudden after the last song James looked out the door and seen her. "Hey, you actually came!" He yelled as he jumped down off the stage. He took his guitar off his shoulder and turned around to hand it to Marcus. Jackie turned around and gave Bridget a very nasty look. James noticed Bridget walking away from the building so he ran outside to catch her while she was leaving. Jackie gave Bridget the feeling as though she wasn't welcome. "Wait, where are you going? I want to talk to you," James called to her. "Ok," Bridget said as she stopped walking so fast. "So, what do you think of our sound? And be honest," He asked her excited. "I think Olivia is right you are amazing and you guys will go far," Bridget said smiling at James trying to forget those sexual feelings she was having just five minutes earlier. "So are you going to the club tonight? I will be there I would like to dance with you," James asked giving Bridget a little smirk. "I don't dance," She said smiling back. "And besides I don't think Jackie would appreciate that." He looked at her raising his eyebrows. "Jackie? She doesn't have any say in what I do. As I said before she is my friend, or are you worried what Jon will think?" James asked while trying to look her in the eye. Bridget kept looking down at the ground in a shy fashion. "No, Jon and I aren't in a relationship anymore. But, I thought you and Jackie were an item?" She paused waiting for his answer. "Jackie and I were an item a few months ago, but I decided I am too young to be so serious," He said as he laughed. "Oh I see," Bridget said in a disappointed way. "So, tonight at the club I won't take no for an answer," He said as he ran back to the building. Bridget watched him run away wondering if she should or shouldn't go to the club that night. She wanted to go so badly, but she had a lot to think about. There were many intense feelings she was going through and she knew things were about to get complicated real fast.

CHAPTER 2

It was down to the wire. Bridget was still debating in her mind if she should go to the club to see James. She felt as though she wasn't good enough for someone as good looking and talented as James seemed to be. Besides, that beauty whom he was seeing was a knockout. Bridget would wonder constantly if he would be thinking of Jackie the whole time he would be with her. "Oh enough!" Bridget shouted. "I am going, what else do I have to lose? I mean he is a friend after all that is all it is." Tina came walking in the living room and laughed, "Who the hell are you talking to?" Bridget turned around quickly and said, "Huh? Nobody lets go to the club! Where is Bev would she like to go too?" Tina looked down at the carpet not wanting to break the news to Bridget. "Look, Bridget, Jon is leaving for the airport tomorrow. He wants to get to L.A as soon as possible," Tina explained. Bridget stopped tying her shoe and looked up at Tina. "So he isn't even going to stay the rest of the summer?" Bridget asked feeling crushed. How could he just leave like this during their last summer together? There were still 3 weeks left of the summer trip. "That is fine, whatever, let him go. I am done with his fickle attitude lately. Let's go to the club!" Bridget said as she rushed out the door in a huff. "Sure, wait up!" Tina yelled. On the way to the club seemed like the longest 15 minutes in the world. When they arrived at the club Bridget walked as fast as her legs could get her in the door. "Will you wait up Bridget, my lord where the hell is the fire?" Tina asked exhausted trying to keep up. When Bridget walked in the door she looked around the club and didn't see who she came to see. "He's not here," Bridget said with sadness to her voice." "Who?" Tina asked curiously. Then came a whisper behind Bridget's right ear. "You made it," James said in his sexy voice. Bridget's heart began to race when she felt his breath on her neck. Tina turned around staring at James with her usual flirtatious manner. "Hi there James, how are you my friend?" Tina asked him with a smile. "Better now, I was wondering if you girls were going to show up," He said walking them over to a table. James offered to buy their drinks as the girls sat down in their seats. "So where is everyone, James? Why are you here alone?" Tina asked. "I'm not alone, Cullen is in the restroom." As soon as James finished his sentence, the song "Crimson and Clover" By Tommy James and the Shondells started to play throughout the club. James looked at the dance floor and then he looked back at Bridget. "So, my dear, care for that dance now?" He asked as he stood up. "Oh, no I told you I don't dance I am lousy at it," She said shaking her head. James reached out and took Bridget's hand and led her to the dance floor. "Come on dancing isn't so bad. Now, come a little bit closer like this," James said as he wrapped his left hand around Bridget's waist and he took her other hand in his. Bridget grabbed James' left shoulder as he pulled her closer. Her eyes came close to his chin and they began to dance. She was so nervous she could feel herself trembling. What if he noticed? Bridget laid her head on his right shoulder as they moved in circles. "This is so nice, see dancing isn't so bad," He whispered in her ear. She felt so comfortable for a change in his arms. Cullen walked up to the table Tina was sitting at. "Wow that is the first time I seen that chick dance the whole time we have been here," Cullen laughed to Tina. "You have no idea she don't dance and I am so shocked she is doing it right now. She must really like him." Tina said watching them dance. Cullen turned to look at them dance as well. "That is a good thing, yes?" Cullen asked. Tina nodded with a small smile. After the song finished James walked with Bridget back to the table. Still standing, he asked Bridget if she would like to go for a walk. She agreed although she was extremely nervous. Why did he want her to go for a walk? She was hoping he wanted to kiss her, but what if he did? She felt awkward about the situation. No man has ever made her feel this way, not even Jon. James grabbed her hand and took her out the door leaving Cullen and Tina to smile at one another wondering what was about to happen. As James and Bridget began to walk they started talking. James began the conversation feeling Bridget's shyness. "This small vacation wasn't what I expected. Hell we just came up here to get away from town for a while. Cobra….." James was speaking as Bridget interrupted him in curiosity, "Cobra?" "Yeah, sorry that is Cullen's nickname since we were kids. His daddy, my uncle Rick, gave him the name on the account of you never knew when he was going to strike when he was pissed off." James giggled as he explained, "Rick even has a cobra tattooed on his left shoulder with the nickname written under it for Cullen." "Sounds like his dad really loves him," Bridget said. "Yes, where I come from family is everything to us. It is very important. We are all extremely close and we do whatever we have to have each other's backs," James explained further. "So what happened with Cullen?" Bridget asked him curiously. "Cullen fell in love with the wrong girl, it was just bad. Things did not end well and that is why we came up here," James spoke with his head down as they walked. Bridget was a little confused. "But, he looks happy. He doesn't look like his heart is broken," She finished. "Looks can be deceiving and we Mackenvoys are good at hiding our feelings. Well, at least some of us are. I don't do too well at it myself," James said with a giggle. Bridget just continued to listen as he spoke intrigued by what he was saying to her. "Cobra is crushed right now and I can't really go into too much detail without scaring you off," James said as he stopped to look at Bridget. "You won't scare me off. I don't know if you could tell, but I really like you James," She said with a small smile. He reached out and pulled her close for a minute and looked into her eyes. She knew it was about to happen. What she had been waiting for all this time. He brought both hands up to her face and cupped it in his hands. He closed his eyes and began to kiss her so passionately. The smell of his breath was sweet and the feel of his tongue in her mouth made her melt. The kiss seemed to last for minutes. She didn't want him to stop. Her legs felt weak and her stomach had butterflies. After he finished kissing her he asked, "Can you feel that?" She did feel what he was talking about. It was magnetic. She felt hypnotized as she looked into his face, the moon shining to light up his beautiful deep eyes. "I want to tell you everything about me, about my family. I want you to know me," He said to her as he rubbed her face with his hand. "I have never felt this strongly before. This past month I have felt so completely different. I will be honest Jackie is amazingly beautiful and sexy, but all I feel when I am with her is lust. I have never felt this desire that I can't explain." He told her as he gently touched her face. Bridget felt intense shyness. James took a step back as he continued to talk to her, "If I am making you uncomfortable I will stop." Bridget spoke up quickly, "No you aren't. I am just nervous because I haven't felt this way either before. I feel like I am in a romance novel," She said giving a little giggle. James laughed and said he felt the same way. "I want to know who you are James. I want to know everything about you if you want to tell me," She said still smiling. James looked at her for a moment and seemed a little uneasy. "If I tell you, you have to promise not to be too judgmental please," He said as he watched her face. "James, I am not that kind of person. I have been judged before and I know how that feels I am nobody to cast stones," She said trying to make him feel more comfortable. He nodded his head, "Ok then I will tell you about my family and about myself. But, not here. For right now we probably should get back to Cullen and Tina. I'm sure they think we have dropped off the face of the earth." James smiled as he grabbed her hand to walk her back to the club. He was a complete gentleman. It showed that he was brought up well and knew how to treat women. He would open doors or pull out chairs for women. In fact Marcus and Cullen behaved in the same manner. Jon was a wonderful man, but he didn't seem to have those gentlemen like qualities. This was foreign to Bridget, but it made her feel like a lady. What a fantastic group of guys she thought. It still nagged at her as to why James seemed so secretive about his family or himself. What could be so bad? If there was anything bad. Bridget couldn't help to notice how sexy James was. It wasn't just his handsome good looks and sexy body, but in the way he spoke and acted was a complete attraction for her. When Bridget and Tina made it home she knew she had to talk to Jon. When they walked into the house Jon was waiting for her. "Where have you been, Bridget?" Jon asked in a stern voice. "Ok, time for me to go to bed," Tina said as she scurried out of the room. "I was at the club," Bridget said softly. "At the club, with him?" Jon asked raising his brow. "Yes, with him and why does it matter you are leaving me anyway?" Bridget raised her voice right back at him. "I told you, I wanted you to come with me. I wanted us to be a couple, but no you can't have that can you? What are you afraid of?" Jon yelled as he stood up to get in her face. "I don't know, I just don't feel like I am good enough! I know you will meet so many beautiful women, Jon." Jon shook his head angrily. "So, you aren't good enough for me, but the goody two shoes Mackenvoy you are? You don't think if he makes it as a rock star you don't have to worry?" He asked her giving her a legitimate question as she paused. "That is different he isn't forced to kiss women, Jon. You will be kissing women and working very closely with them there is a big difference. There are a lot of rock stars who are faithful to their women," Bridget said as she began to get upset. Jon began to pace back and forth then he asked, "You know what I think? I think you never felt as deeply for me as you thought you did." Bridget just stared down at the floor. "I am leaving tomorrow. I know now that is for the best," Jon said while he stomped out of the room. Bridget felt empty and terrible. She never wanted to hurt Jon, but that is exactly what she had done. At that moment her thoughts went back to James. Maybe Jon was right, what guarantee would she have that James would be faithful? She doesn't really know him and Jon she has known for two years. In life you take risks and there are no guarantees. She thought at that moment to plunge in with both feet, to see where this goes with James. But, would this be the biggest mistake of her life?

CHAPTER 3

The morning was warm as Jon gathered his clothes together to leave for the airport. Their goodbye was difficult, but also awkward under the circumstances. Bridget was going to miss him. He was an important part of her life for a long time. But, she still couldn't get James off of her mind. For the next two weeks their relationship became intensely serious. However, Bridget made the decision not to escalate it. They had not made love yet although the chemistry was very intense between them. She wanted it to be right and most important she wanted to be sure he was interested in her for who she was and not just sex. James was very affectionate and kind with her. She would go to watch their band play when they would have practices. Jackie would also be there which would make it very awkward for Bridget. Soon Jackie had a moment to talk to Bridget alone. "So, you and James seem to be heating things up," She said in a pushy nosy way. "Yes but, we are taking things slow. I am sorry if things didn't work out between the two of you," Bridget said kindly. Jackie smiled and said, "He will get bored with you soon you will see. And he and I will get back to where we left off. Honestly, do you really think that he would be interested in something romantic with someone like you? I mean, it's obvious you are after his money and Victoria won't stand for that." Bridget became angry and snapped back, "I don't know what you are talking about. I have no clue who Victoria is and I had no idea he had money. I could really care less about that. I am not materialistic," Bridget finished in a huff. "Right that is what they all say isn't it? Poor people I mean like you," Jackie flipped around and walked off feeling as though she accomplished the goal she was aiming for. The conversation left Bridget feeling sick to her stomach. She had fallen in love with James, but now what? She didn't know anything really about his life. They hadn't had a chance to talk about that. They were too involved in the good time they were having together. Bridget never thought to ask him about what he was wanting to tell her that night at the club. After the bands practice ended Bridget walked up to James and told him she had to talk to him and it was important. Jackie sat back and smiled knowing things should change soon. Bridget brought James back to her house since Tina and Bev would be out for the rest of the day. "Ok, so what is it you need to talk about?" James asked her as he sat down directly in front of her. "Jackie told me someone named Victoria wouldn't stand for me and you being together," Bridget said as she watched James stand up and give out a long sigh. Rubbing his hand through his hair he began to explain, "Victoria is my mother. Jackie may have seemed like a bitch to you, but she is right. My momma is going to make things a little rough for us." Bridget shook her head in disbelief, "If you knew your mom wouldn't like someone like me then what do you want from me, James? Are you playing games with me? Was your whole intent to have a summer fling?" James walked over to Bridget and grabbed both her arms in his hands. "No, I didn't want….. I was wanting to see how I felt about you before I explained everything to you," He said trying to keep her gaze. Bridget pushed his hands away. "Well I am all ears now. Will you please tell me? I am feeling like I am in deep now and I want to know what I am getting involved in," She said forcefully. James walked

8

over to the window. As he looked outside he began telling her all about his family. "We are a powerful family in Tennessee, but we aren't the only powerful family. There is another family that lives there. We hate them, they hate us. We all get made fun of by some people comparing us all to a family in history that used to fight as well, but we are not like them. Except for the fact that we don't want any of our family members mixing and that is where the similarities end. I do have money, my daddy is very rich. His granddad had an oil business that has been handed down to my daddy, we are originally from Texas. My momma comes from a wealthy family as well. I know you aren't after my money because you had no idea that I was rich. Ignore anything Jackie says about that." Bridget listened as he explained, but feeling a bit foolish for not learning about all this sooner. She had to ask him again, "If your family has a problem with you dating someone of limited means then why did you get involved with me?" James turned around to look at her. "My daddy has nothing against anyone with no money, my momma is the one who can be a bit frigid about it. We give to all kinds of charities. Trust me Bridget, we are good people. We don't look down on anybody. And besides this isn't about what they want for me it should be what I want for me now!" He said getting a little emotional. "Well, except your momma," Bridget snapped. "She just don't want me involved with someone who hasn't come from a prominent family. My momma's social status is very important to her, but not everyone else in my family is like that. You met my cousin and brother," He finished speaking just looking at her. "I see, so tell me about Cullen. You were going to tell me something about him awhile back?" She asked waiting for his answer. James sat back down in front of Bridget. "Cullen was involved with a girl named Rachel. The problem was, her last name was Hillenbrand. Which means she was a member of the other family. These are the rich powerful people we hate. Cullen and Rachel hid their relationship and Rachel became pregnant, the Hillenbrand family blew up. They were so pissed at my cousin. Cullen told Rachel he couldn't be with her on the account of the family issues. Rachel didn't agree. She wanted to be with him no matter what the family thought. She wanted to run away with him and start a life, but he couldn't leave us. Rachel ended up taking a bottle of sleeping pills." Bridget interrupted him in shock, "She died? Oh my god, that is horrible!" James continued to explain, "Yes, she died and now the Hillenbrands only blame Cullen. And what is even worse is he did exactly what they wanted him to do, he left her alone. When he did she just fell apart." Bridget was wondering at this moment what she was getting into. James reached out and grabbed her face, "I need you to understand that I am crazy about you. I have never felt this way before about anyone. I need to know you are willing to give me a chance. I wasn't hiding anything from you. I told you that night at the club I planned on telling you all about me and my family. Please, don't dump me over this. My family are good people. We are just a little intense at times." Bridget let out a laugh and asked, "Intense? You are talking about an overbearing mother and a suicide. What am I supposed to think about this? And why do you call them momma and daddy?" She asked him in a silly type of voice. James didn't answer her and began kissing her passionately. He didn't want to ruin what they had before it had even started so he said, "I'm crazy about you and I want us to have a shot at this. Can you give me that? Just a chance to prove to you that I am a good man." Bridget couldn't resist kissing him. James stopped kissing her to take off his shirt and Bridget stared at his slightly hairy muscular chest. The hair was fine and straight as she ran her fingers through it, it felt soft to her touch. James picked her up and carried her to the bedroom. Laying her down gently on the bed, he continued to kiss her mouth and her neck. He whispered to her, "I love you." While he looked deep into her eyes. "I love you too, James, so much." He gave her a big smile and began kissing her deeply again. Licking her lips and sliding his tongue into her mouth. She could feel the butterflies fluttering in her stomach. She reached down to feel him through his pants and was shocked when she realized James was not a small guy.

She let out a small gasp and said, "James?" "Yes," He whispered. "I am a little afraid this is a little overwhelming," She said holding back on her kissing. James put his finger on her mouth to stop her from talking and he whispered, "I will be as gentle as you need me to be. I won't force anything on you and I don't want to hurt you in anyway." She didn't say a word and began kissing him again. Moving her way down his neck. The smell of his cologne wasn't over bearing, it was perfect just as he was to her. His chest was really chiseled as was his abs. She could tell he worked out frequently. She continued to rub his body while they took each other in. James moved his way down to her chest and belly, licking and kissing her gently. He occasionally would glance up at her to make sure she was ok with what he was doing. He moved farther down and as he kissed her lower belly he began sliding her panties down her thighs. After taking her panties completely off, he gently laid his nose on her to take in her smell for a moment. He gently licked the outside and she began to moan. He pleasured her as she felt herself starting to feel a little shy from the moans she was making. She felt intense desire for him and she began to let herself go. As he tasted her he looked up at her, watching her as she squirmed around enjoying his touch. Grabbing her hips as he buried his face, he could feel her pulsate. She ran her fingers through his hair while he continued to pleasure her. When he was finished he raised up and looked her in the eyes as he began to slide into her. Wrapping his hand around the back of her neck he gently pushed inside her with gentle thrusts. She pressed her nails into his chest as he tried to enter her completely. She let out a loud moan as he moved in and out of her, their breaths both becoming quicker and louder. James managed to make her feel things she hadn't up until that point. The feeling was intense and real to her. He made her lose her inhibitions every time she would climax. They made love while they gazed into each other's eyes. When he started to get closer to his release, he became a little rougher causing her to have trouble catching her breath. She started to get louder as he tensed up, grabbing her hair while he came inside of her. He moaned as he tried to catch his breath. Laying down beside her they began kissing again. "Are you ok?" He asked wiping the sweat off her forehead. "Yes, I am happy." She smiled as they fell asleep in each other's arms.

CHAPTER 4

"Oh my god!" Tina said in a loud voice as James and Bridget jerked awake. James looked around with his eyes half shut forgetting for a brief second where he was at. "Oh shit, where's my clothes?" He said looking around grabbing all his clothing off the floor. "Looking for this?" Tina smiled holding up his shirt. He gave an embarrassed look and yanked the shirt from her hand. "Babe, I got to go," He said giving Bridget a long kiss. "I will see you soon," She said as he scurried out the front door. "Bye, James!" Tina and Beverly said in a joking fashion. "Alright, come on enough with the teasing," Bridget said embarrassed herself. "So, how was it?" Beverly asked with excitement. "Big," Bridget replied with a half-smile walking off to the bathroom. Both Tina and Beverly looked at each other with their mouths wide open. "I never would have guessed he is only 5 foot 9 inches isn't he? Aren't guys who are well hung taller?" Tina asked. "No that is just a stereotype and not necessarily true," Beverly said laughing. Bridget jumped in the shower with a smile on her face as she washed herself. Thinking about James the whole time. She wanted to call him so badly. She already missed him and he was only gone for 5 minutes. James jumped in his car and headed back to his place. Smelling his skin after being with Bridget and thinking about her as well. He isn't the boasting type. Which is why she never knew how big his lower member was. That is one thing about himself he prided himself on when he is with women, but he doesn't use it as a tool to get women. James was very well endowed and any woman he was with was intimidated by it at first. He tends to be teased a lot by his band mates, but he just over looks it. And maybe he does rub that fact in their faces, what man wouldn't? Born in 1982, he was the middle son of Colton and Victoria Mackenvoy. He is a huge romantic at heart, but he is also a lion when he is protecting what is his. He can be a bit hot headed at times without thinking before acting. Marcus, James' older brother, was a sexy man himself. With short dark hair and deep dark eyes, he was a charmer. Being two years older than James, he was born in 1980. He had to protect his brother and baby sister, Emma, from harm. He used his smarts more than muscle. Never looking for a fight, but could fight when it was warranted. He is more of a lover than a fighter. His body was nicely chiseled and not too overly muscular. Completely faithful to the current woman in his life, Olivia. He met her during his second year of college. Her beautiful green eyes are what caught his attention and has kept him hooked ever since. Olivia comes from an influential family which makes their relationship a bonus to his mother, Victoria. Attending law school, Marcus' goal is to work in family and business law. Working for the family business is in his future, but he loves being in the band with James, Cullen and Matt. Bass guitar has been his passion for most of his teenage life. He sings backup vocals and leaves most of the lyrical work to James. Marcus, James and Cullen all agreed they wanted to make it as a band all on their own, without the help of their fathers' money. The guys had been in their band since their early teens. Matt has always been around the Mackenvoys. In fact, it is a running joke that he was adopted by them since he has been a big part of their lives. Matt is the same age as James. He met Cindy while she was working in an ice cream shop. He couldn't resist her adorable brown eyes and her cute short strawberry blonde hair. The way she tied her hair back in the pony tail melted his heart. He stood 6 foot tall while she was a mere 5 foot 3 inches. He never had many ambitions except for music and working as a carpenter in odd jobs. It came in handy when he helped out the Mackenvoys with their charitable work. Charity was very important to the Mackenvoys. They would donate to several charities along with aiding in any type of natural disaster help. The family is, in fact, very powerful and rich. Cullen Mackenvoy is the first cousin to Marcus and James. Born in 1980, he was an impressive 6 foot 2 inches with a muscular build. A very cunning type of mind, but also one of the best fighters in their town. Fighting was another important part of their family's life, as Bridget would soon find out. Cullen also attends college going for his business degree to pursue his career with the family business. All the Mackenvoy boys were being groomed for their places in the family oil business. But, during this summer James' mind wasn't on college or his family's business. The feelings he began having for Bridget struck him like a lightning bolt from the sky. Meeting her in that café was a turning point for him. When James arrived back at the house it was very late. Everyone else was already in bed. He sat down and thought about Bridget for a while. Wondering if he wanted to get her involved with his family. He knew how he felt about her, but he also knew how his mother could be. Victoria Mackenvoy came from a very rich family so she had very high expectations. She would give to charity gladly like her husband, but she didn't want someone she considered an unfortunate in her family. Colton Mackenvoy and his brother Rick, Cullen's father, were not this way. They didn't look down on others for not having wealth. They were stern fathers. Raising their boys to be strong smart men, it was all on the account of the family they were enemies with. Everything was a competition. Victoria had a certain idea of what kind of woman was best for James. He was not a momma's boy, but he did always want to please her. He already knew Bridget would not make her happy. She was thrilled when James and Jackie began dating. Jackie also came from money and she was the equivalent to a super model. She was 5 foot 5 inches tall with beautiful dark wavy hair and big blue eyes. Her figure was slender with sexy breast implants to finish off her look. There wasn't an ounce of fat on her frame or smidgen of cellulite anywhere on her body, she seen to that. She was the type of girl who wouldn't leave the house without makeup on her face and her hair done up properly. She was madly in love with James. So much so she was certain he would propose to her, but that summer things didn't go as planned. James and Jackie were taking a break as a couple, but still took the trip together as friends. She was hoping to reconcile so she seen Bridget as a huge problem. Bridget to Jackie was a humiliation if James preferred her over Jackie. What did this Bridget have that she didn't after all? Jackie thought of herself as much more beautiful and had so much more to offer James. That night Jackie waited up for James alone in her bed, but she fell asleep before he came home. He walked to her room and seen her sound asleep, instead of waking her he walked over to the couch and sat down. He sat on the couch knowing he would have to explain to Jackie there was not going to be a reconciliation. How could he though? He didn't want to hurt her, he cared a lot for her. He thought he did love her at one time. But, there was always something missing. In Bridget, everything seemed complete. She had everything he had ever wanted, except his mother's approval. Money was not an issue for James. He was such a romantic and he had been looking for a woman like Bridget his whole life. He knew his father wouldn't have a problem with her as long as James was happy with her. Although, Victoria was a force to be reckoned with. If she wasn't happy, then nobody would be safe from her wrath. In a way, James was a little jealous of Marcus and Olivia's romance. Victoria bragged continuously of their relationship to anyone who would listen. She had done the same for James and Jackie, but James wasn't in love with Jackie the way Marcus was with Olivia. Marcus and Olivia were getting married that September, they both were hiding a small secret. All James wanted was to feel that passionate love for someone, to want to actually marry someone. He hadn't felt this type of desire yet, until Bridget. True he was only 18 years old at the time, but in this particular family you did marry young and have your own kids at a young age. His dad and uncle were both 20 years old when they had their first child in 1980. This was the year 2000 and James was ready for his life to change. The year seemed special to him. He knew his father would be so happy that he found someone. Colton was ready for both of his boys to marry and make him a granddad at the young age of 40. But, still it was all about his mother and Bridget still didn't know everything. She had no idea how brutal these two families were to each other. If she decided to give her life with James a chance, she would find out. The Mackenvoy's nemesis was the Hillenbrands. A powerful wealthy architecture family who lived in the same town as the Mackenvoys. The feeling of hatred was entirely mutual between both families. The whole state of Tennessee knew all about these two families and soon the whole world would as well. The feud between the two families started over a silly spat between Colton and the head of the Hillenbrand family, Packard. There was no bad blood earlier on in these family's lives, it all started here. Packard Hillenbrand came from a rich family and their expertise was architecture. When Colton and Packard were in Junior high the trouble began. Colton and Rick moved to Tennessee from Texas during their early teens. Immediately, Colton and Packard never liked one another and it spilled over onto both of their brothers. Packard had an older brother named Walter and a younger brother named Jackson. Still, Rick Mackenvoy was the biggest strongest one of them all. Packard and Jackson couldn't stand the Mackenvoy brothers because they were just as rich as the Hillenbrands were. It was all about power between both of the men. By the time the boys were in High School the fights were intense between them all. Rick was muscular and smart, being on the wrestling team he did a good job at beating all the Hillenbrand boys. When Colton met the love of his life, Lisa, Packard had always had a deep passion for her, but never acted on it. Packard couldn't stand the thought of someone like Colton walking into his town and stealing a girl from him. Colton had Lisa wrapped around his finger, but that didn't stop Packard from trying to win her heart. Many things happened to lead up to Packard stealing Lisa away from Colton. This is how the war began between the two families. Packard was a notorious man who didn't mind toeing the line of breaking the law to get what he wanted. Colton paid a heavy price when he went up against Packard in a blood soaked fight that nearly ended Colton's life. Lisa didn't want to see Colton hurt any worse than what he was so she made her choice to stay with Packard. Eventually Colton met Victoria, but she was no Lisa. He still carried the flame for Lisa which irritated Victoria. Lisa had a kind heart and a soft side to her whereas Victoria was rough and uptight. They both looked totally different as well. Lisa was short with blonde hair and green eyes, while Victoria was somewhat tall with dark curly hair and dark eyes. Lisa was similar to Bridget in a lot of ways which is one thing that would make it difficult for them to be a couple with Victoria being involved. She despised Lisa, so if James brought home a girl very similar to Lisa and with no wealthy means it would be enough to send Victoria into a rage. James was all too aware of this fact, but he wanted Bridget so badly. As he sat and thought of all the problems that lie ahead, he drifted off to sleep on the sofa.

CHAPTER 5

The next morning was raining hard outside. James was still sleeping on the sofa when everyone else began to wake up. Jackie came out of her room wiping the sleep from her eyes. She seen James sleeping soundly in his clothes with his forearm cradled under his face. She sat down on the table in front of him and just stared at his peaceful face. "I love you, dummy," She whispered when all the sudden she heard Cullen come in to the room. "Morning Cobra," Jackie said. "Morning, Miss Jackie. How are you this rainy morning?" Cullen asked her grabbing a bowl to pour his cereal in. Just then James started to wake up, stretching and moaning as he was rubbing his eyes. "So, where were you last night so late?" Jackie asked him hoping she would get a silly answer about a flat tire. "I was visiting someone," He tiredly told her. "Visiting someone? Would this someone have blonde frizzy hair?" Jackie rudely asked. "Jackie, please don't start already this morning." He said raising up into a sitting position. Jackie raised her voice to James, "Just answer the fucking question, did you go to see her?" He paused for a minute knowing what he was about to say would hurt her. "Yes I did," He said looking sternly at her face, "I went to talk to her privately because you couldn't keep your mouth shut. So I had to explain a few things to her." "Oh, and how did she take it? I am assuming she was fine with everything since you stayed so long…." Jackie jumped up very upset and turned her back to him. Cullen was sitting at the table crunching on his cereal and listening to their conversation. Marcus and Olivia came walking into the kitchen wondering what all the yelling was about. In the background everyone could hear Matt and Cindy making love, but everyone seemed to ignore that. All they cared about was what was going on in front of them. Marcus sat down with a bowl of cereal as well while Olivia stood watching Jackie. She walked over to Jackie and touched her arm. "Are you ok honey?" Olivia asked. Jackie sobbed, "I am not ok nothing is ok. How can you throw away what we have?" She asked looking at James. He just sat with his head down not knowing what to say to her. Olivia looked over at James while trying to comfort Jackie. "What is going on? Where were you?" Olivia asked a little confused. "I was at Bridget's house. I think it is safe to say that she and I are wanting to take things to the next level. And I am so sorry, Jackie, if this hurts you. But, why would you want to be with someone who doesn't give you what you need?" James asked her gently trying to touch her arm. "Don't touch me!" Jackie shouted crying hysterically and ran from the room. Olivia tried to be comforting, but nothing she said worked. Olivia had a kind gentle way to her. She had a very soft sweet voice that was very soothing. She had a way of making people feel better and she always tried to see the bright side of a situation. In this case she really didn't know what to say. "James, I just don't understand." Olivia said walking up to him. James flopped back down on the couch and said, "What is there to not understand? I don't love Jackie, she deserves much better than that. I want to feel what I am feeling right now for someone and it isn't Jackie. Why can't anyone understand that?" James was starting to feel angry as to why nobody understood. Marcus stood up putting his bowl in the sink. "I get it brother, don't worry about it we will work through this. She will understand just give her time," Marcus said in an assured way. "I really hope you are right Marcus," James said as he walked to the bathroom to take his shower. "Oh Marcus, this is bad. I mean, I don't know this Bridget chick too well, but I know Jackie is crazy about him. Oh god and Victoria is going to literally have a cow!" Olivia said feeling very concerned. Matt and Cindy came walking into the kitchen looking at everyone wondering what was going on. Cullen stood up to get ready for the day himself. "Look everyone if he doesn't love Jackie he is right, what is the point in being with someone you don't love? I think Victoria is the one who loves Jackie, not James. And it isn't fair forcing him to be with someone he doesn't want to be with," Cullen said as he left the room brushing past Matt and Cindy. "What the hell is going on?" Cindy asked confused. Olivia explained what she knew to them both, but everyone was still at a loss as to what to do next for Jackie. Jackie was obviously crazy about James and he wasn't about her. What could anyone do to help? Cindy wasn't afraid to give her opinion on the matter. She was the type who would tell people what she thought no matter what others thought of her. Cindy felt as though it should all be James' decision. After being around the Mackenvoys for the past year she realized how much of a tyrant Victoria really was. It made her sick how she tried to rule all her kids' lives. Matt would tell her to keep that stuff to herself, but this time she wouldn't hold her tongue. As soon as James came out of the shower Cindy rushed up to him to give him her advice on the whole matter. Matt begged her to stay out of it. But, she just couldn't. She was just so sad seeing how unhappy James was and it was time for him to find what he was looking for. Cullen and even Marcus had to agree with her. She told James to just follow his heart no matter what anyone else thought and that is supposed to be his life. He should live it for himself. He has been ruled by his parents until now. He is 18 years old and it is time to find what makes him happy in life. James knew what he had to do and he was going to do it. He had never felt this way before and he was going to see where it took him. He believed if his momma cared for him, she would understand and want what was best for him. James couldn't wait any longer he called Bridget's cell phone. When she answered he asked if he could see her. On his way over to her house the rain hit his windshield and he couldn't help but feel a sense of freedom. He had extreme excitement filling his chest as he pulled up to her house. He also tried to control himself since he was starting to feel aroused again just thinking about what had happened the night before. He rushed up to the door and knocked loudly. When she opened the door she smiled slyly. Her hair was back in a messy ponytail, but she looked so adorable to him. Very wholesome and down to earth. This was one of the things he loved so much about her. She could pull off the no makeup look very well, it suited her. As soon as he walked in the front door he cupped her face in his hands and gave her a long kiss not paying attention to the giggles in the background of Beverly and Tina. Trying to control himself, he backed up and asked her how her sleep was. She let him know she slept like a baby. All the while there was snickering in the background. Bridget asked James if he would like to go for a walk to have some privacy. He smiled and agreed. "See you later, ladies!" James shouted in the door. As they walked down the sidewalk he grabbed her hand in his and started to talk to her, "So, how do you feel about what happened last night?" He looked over to her. "I'm ok with it, I am just a little nervous about this whole thing. I haven't had a chance to feel so passionately about someone. Jon and I had a great relationship. I just couldn't let myself fall completely in love with him. I just felt like I wouldn't be good enough for him. After a while I am sure he would meet someone much better than me." James looked at her with a puzzled look on his face. "Why do you have such a low self-esteem of yourself? You are beautiful," He said as he smiled. "Oh my god, are you blind?" Bridget said laughing. "No I am not blind, I know what I see. And I see someone I would love to get to know better. Which brings me to what I was wanting to ask you. It is a lot to ask I know this, but I really need to know if you are the one for me," James was still thinking of the words he was wanting to use when she spoke up. "I want you to ask me anything you want to. We need to get used to asking tough questions," She said with a serious tone. "Ok, here goes then. I would like you to move down to Tennessee so we are closer to one another. I will pay for a house for you to rent just so you don't have to worry about anything," He blurted it all out quickly stunning her. Bridget stopped walking in a bit of a shock. James knew it would be a little bit of a shock for her, but he wanted to get to know her and would that be possible living nearly 5 hours away from each other? Bridget stared at the sidewalk for a few seconds and then raised her head, "I don't know what to say. I mean I want to get to know you too and see where this goes, but first off I am not one who takes handouts. And second I would be moving away from my family and friends." James felt a little sad with how she was seeing things. "I don't see this as me giving you a handout, I see this as me helping you relocate your life for me. I am not trying to buy you off if that is what you think?" He said watching her uneasiness. Bridget thought for a moment, "James, I need to think about this please. I am so scared to do this. I mean, we have been friends now for almost three months and dating for two weeks, but I am just scared do you understand?" James put his arms around her and said, "Yes I understand sweetheart. I just don't know any other way. I am starting my first year of accounting classes and the band is working hard so we can buy some studio time. I just know I want to be with you. And I am sure this will work." Bridget thought for a moment and for the first time she felt as though she was ready to make a decision without analyzing it to death. "Yes, I will move down there," She said squeezing her eyes shut. James was all excited and grabbed her up into his arms. He kissed her several times while he was talking, "You will? You said you will? I am so happy, baby, I am so fucking happy really. Oh shit I am sorry I have been trying my best not to be crude with the language!" Bridget couldn't help but laugh at his silliness. He wasn't aware that she herself could be crude as well when she was upset. This was one of the biggest decision Bridget would ever make in her life. She had no idea what lay in store for her.

CHAPTER 6

Heading back to her hometown in Indiana, Bridget talked to Beverly and Tina about her plans to move to Tennessee for a while. Of course, her friends relayed their concern for their best friend. Bridget is aware she doesn't know anyone in that state but, she also knows she has never felt so strongly for a man before like she did that summer with James. She was afraid to uproot her life and leave her family and friends. But, she couldn't help to wonder if this was the man she was meant to be with. It was worth it to at least see where this would go. If anything she could always move back home it was only 5 hours away. When they arrived in their hometown each went back to their own homes, exhausted from the long trip. James was to arrive at Bridget's home in a few days to meet her family as she would explain her drastic decision to move away. It was now the beginning of September and the fall semester would be starting soon. Beverly was all excited to be enrolled in dental school. Tina and Bridget still had no idea of what they were wanting to do with their lives. All that seemed to be on Bridget's mind lately was James. When he came to her parent's house that hot late summer day everyone seemed to be on edge. Bridget's parents, Robert and Patty Case, were extremely nice people. Rob worked hard to raise his family but was seldom home. He never had time for his children let alone Patty. She accepted that this was her life and promised to stand by her husband. Patty had a silly sense of humor and she could be a little aloof at times. Bridget kept to herself as a child growing up but, she always wanted to be something great. Sophia, Bridget's younger sister, was the baby of the family. She was the one her parents knew would be someone special. Bridget was never jealous of her sister in anyway. In fact, she didn't mind Sophia had all eyes on her. It took the focus off Bridget. Her older brother, Greg, had a hard time with life. He had a bit of a drug problem, but was one of the greatest men you could meet. This is why Bridget felt safe to move away from home. Family life could seem rough for her at times and getting away with James felt like a new beginning. James seemed to enjoy the company of her family. He did try to explain to them how his family was a little different, but he promised that Bridget would be taken care of if she moved down there to be with him. After the long visit with Bridget's parents, she and James packed up all her belongings and jumped in her car to head down south. James had a plan on their way there. Even though it wasn't a long trip, he rented a big cabin in the Kentucky hills for the night. He wanted this time alone with her, completely alone. When they pulled up to the cabin Bridget was a little surprised. He wanted her to be. He asked her to wait out in the car as he went into the cabin. She waited for about 15 minutes noticing that it was starting to get late. They had left Indiana around 6:00pm and it was coming up on 9:30pm. James came out to the car with a sly smile on his face. "Ok, my dear, it is time to come in and relax." He opened the car door for her as she walked up the steps to go into the cabin. He ran in front of her asking her to wait a moment so he could open the door. When she stepped in all she seen was lit candles everywhere. It was a beautiful cabin. He led her to a small kitchen table where there was peanut butter sandwiches, strawberries and champagne. "Now, don't make fun of the meal. I couldn't exactly bring steak I think it would have gotten a little bad on the trip and I wanted this to be a surprise," He said pulling out her chair for her. Bridget just smiled as she sat down in her seat. "This is totally fine and so sweet of you to do this," She said as she took a bite of her sandwich. James began pouring their champagne in their glasses as he spoke to her in a sexy way, "I think this is probably the first date we have ever had. Even though we dated around in Canada, I don't feel like I gave you a proper evening. So this is to make up for that and my apology all at the same time." They both gave a little giggle. And James became serious, "But, really I want tonight to be very special for us. I kind of feel as though our first time felt rushed and I am so sorry for that." Bridget shook her head. "It is ok, I wasn't expecting it to be like a fairytale," She said smiling at James. "Yes, it should feel like that. I am slacking in my romancing with you and that stops now. You deserve to be treated like a lady, so that is what I am going to do," He said with a determined tone to his voice. They had a quiet dinner and began to know one another much better. After dinner James grabbed her by the hand and led her to an outside deck where there was a warm hot tub with candles all around it. "I realize we don't have bathing suits, or maybe you do but it is in the mess in the back of your car," James said laughing. He walked up to her pulling her shirt up over her head. "But, I thought maybe we could take a relaxing swim anyway," He whispered as he took her shirt off. He pulled his shirt off as well. Reaching down he unzipped her jean shorts and took them off slowly. She unzipped his khaki shorts and slid her hand down the back of his shorts so she could feel inside his underwear. She grabbed his butt cheeks in her hands as she moved in to kiss his neck. He closed his eyes as he started to grab her butt as well and he gave it a strong squeeze. She licked up his neck and licked his lips gently. She could feel his erection poking her left thigh as he pressed himself against her. She began having strong feelings of complete intense desire for him. The feeling of being weak in the knees was so powerful she thought she was going to collapse. She felt his strong hard shoulders as he began kissing her hard on the lips. Opening her mouth to let his tongue slide inside hers. They stopped kissing for a moment so they could look deep into each other's eyes. It was hypnotic. She backed up and began to take her bra off. James swallowed hard as he looked at her body, which to him seemed perfect in every way. She would always notice little imperfections, but he didn't see this. All he seen was beauty. She slipped her panties down to her ankles and stepped out of them. Every inch of her amazed him as he took her in. She started to feel a little modest and began to cover her private area. James shook his head and walked over to her saying, "Let me see." He brushed her hands away and she stared at his face as he looked down at her most intimate parts. He gently caressed her breasts and put his lips to them as he continued to rub her body. She could feel herself getting hot and very turned on. He kneeled down on his knees and began to taste her. She threw her head back and made a gasp sound. She was feeling extremely excited and sensitive. His tongue felt almost too good. In her mind she was going crazy wanting to eat this man alive. She ran her fingers through his hair as he continued to lick her, sending chills throughout her body. She backed up and whispered, "Now it is your turn. Take them off." He stood up wiping his face with his hand. He slid his pants and underwear off and stepped out of them. She looked down feeling her face get a little red and said, "Wow it is as impressive as I thought it was going to be." He just smiled. She walked slowly over to him and dropped down to her knees. Looking up at him she took a deep breath and opened her mouth to take as much of him in as she possibly could. He grabbed her hair with his fist and moaned as she moved him in and out of her mouth. As she continued to play with him in her mouth he whispered trying to catch his breath, "Stop, babe, you've got to stop or we can't do what we really want to do." Standing up she smiled with a smirk. He started to walk toward her, but she backed up and stepped down into the hot tub. He came in after her and grabbed her up in his arms. They began passionately kissing as he pulled her up onto his lap. She felt him start to slide in her as she squeezed her eyes shut moaning out in pain and pleasure when he gave a thrust deep inside her. She tensed herself all around him, he wasn't holding back this time. They both moaned as he pushed his hips upward. She whispered in his ear for him not to stop and he didn't. He just kept on pumping harder and faster until neither could hold back anymore. Not wanting to stop he fought it as long as he could, but Bridget wasn't used to the size of him. She whispered, "Come on baby let me have it." He threw his head back and moaned as he exploded deep inside of her. When they were finished making love they cradled each other in the hot tub and kissed slowly. "I love you, I can feel it. You are my girl I have been looking for." He said looking her deep in the eyes. Bridget stared back at him for a moment and let him know how scared she was. For this was all new to her. He assured her they would be okay if she would trust him. The next morning as they were getting ready for the last few hours of the trip James thought of something he hadn't thought of before. "You know, I never asked you a very important question," He said eyeing her intently. "What is that?" She asked. "Birth control? We haven't been using any and I was just curious. Not that I wouldn't mind a baby with you. I know we need to know each other better first," He said with a small giggle. "I agree, yes I am on birth control you don't have to worry about that. I wouldn't trap anyone like that," She said as she started to walk out the door. "No, I knew you wouldn't do that, baby. I just wanted to know to make sure I wasn't doing things the wrong way. I really do want this to work," James said following her out the door. "I do too. I am so excited to meet your family. I think Marcus and Cullen are great I am sure the rest of your family are the same way." James' mind wondered to his overbearing mother. Bridget was so ready to get back in the car and get to their destination. James, however, was much more nervous. He knew everyone else was accepting, but it was his mother, just his mother.

CHAPTER 7

Pulling into the small modest town of Pleasantville, Bridget looked around to take in the sights of the new place she was to call home. It was a nice little town, not full of hustle and bustle. It did have the standard grocery stores, gas stations and nice restaurants. She was so excited to get to know this new place. James drove around town showing her the different places they typically go to get coffee or food. He drove all the way through town and then stopped at the road that heads west out of town. "Now, this road here obviously takes you out of town. But, it also takes you out in the country around the neighborhood of the Hillenbrands," James explained. "The Hillenbrands?" Bridget asked confused. "Sounds mysterious," She said laughing. James stared down the road quiet for a moment. The he looked at her after taking off his sunglasses, "The Hillenbrands are our biggest enemies here in this town. We hate each other. It is a long story I will tell you soon, but basically it started between our father and the Hillenbrand boys' father. It was really stupid I guess you could say. Over a woman like it usually is." Bridget laughed, "Oh now blame the poor lady of the situation." Staring at James acting uneasy she suddenly felt a little concerned. "James, how bad is this? You are acting way too strange," She said as she watched him stare off. "It is bad enough where we fight, I mean really fight. We don't hold back. If one of us pisses the other off we go at it until there is blood. Sometimes a lot of blood. We never press charges or call cops, we aren't pussies. We are all tough and we take our whippings," He paused giving her a minute to take it all in. She looked down the road that had him so serious acting and felt a little confused. She felt as though she was in a movie watching herself and she started to feel a little tricked. "So, you got me here over false pretenses?" She asked. James was shocked, "Whoa, wait no…no I never did that. I told you I would explain all about us. That is what I am doing. I never deceived you in any way. I am just trying to tell you about this family that we don't get along with." Bridget became frustrated and raised her voice, "You could have told me this shit before you dragged me all the way down here. I mean, what if I didn't want to be a part of this? The way you talk it is everyday life. Not just a little spat here and there." James felt like he may have just lost the best thing that happened to him, "I am sorry I didn't tell you before bringing you here, but maybe I was afraid you wouldn't give me a chance if you knew. It isn't as bad as it sounds. We are good people really we are. We just don't get along with them." Bridget interrupted very upset, "But, you are telling me these unsavory people live right down this road like something out of a mob movie." James giggled. "What, you think this is funny?" She snapped. "No I don't think it is funny it just sounded funny. They aren't like the mob. We don't try to kill one another. We just try to show who is better or put each other in their place," He finished staring at her. "Oh well that sums everything up and makes total sense," She said sarcastically. James let out a sigh and looked back out the car window. "Look, if you don't want any part of me or this situation just tell me. I will take you back to Indiana and I won't put you through meeting my family. But, I really do want to see where this goes, please. I am just asking for a chance. We aren't crazy. We try to give to whatever charities we can and help out with disaster relief and so does the Hillenbrands. We just hate each other, you are safe honest," James said as Bridget stared down the road. "Safe....... ok I will stick with you since you said there is nothing super violent I have to worry about," She said reluctantly as James smiled and started kissing her. Then she pulled away for a second and looked him in the eye. "But, the first sign of craziness and I am gone I mean that," She finished. "Ok that is fair," He said continually kissing her happily. "Ok, so now it is time to get you over to the house I rented and then later we will go to my parents picnic they are having it at their house," He told her as he started the car. Bridget was feeling very nervous now. James turned the car around and started to go back through town. He turned down a dead end street and there sat a small cute house. She was happy to spend the upcoming months here. They took all her belongings into the house. It was a two bedroom house with one floor, but very peaceful and quiet sitting at the end of cul-de-sac. It was now 1:00pm on this humid September afternoon and it was about time to head to the Mackenvoy's manor for the family get together. James explained that he, Marcus and little sister Emma all still lived at the manor with their parents at the moment. With Marcus and Olivia's wedding coming up fast, he would be moving out of the manor to be with his wife. Marcus had to start his third year of law school and he was ready to get his life going. Marcus was very ambitious. And there was a small secret being kept among the family. Apparently, Olivia was already going on four months of pregnancy with Marcus' baby. Bridget wasn't aware of the pregnancy yet. After getting her things settled, James and Bridget jumped back in the car to head over to the Mackenvoy manor. They left town in the opposite direction of the Hillenbrand road. Traveling about 15 miles outside of Pleasantville in a southeast direction she noticed the landscape was similar to Indiana. She did feel at home even though she didn't have her family or old friends here. But, all the sudden she thought about Jon. She wondered how he was doing. If he was okay and if he was settling in California alright. She debated on calling his cell phone to see how he was. She decided she would do just that the next day when she had some time. Arriving at the manor Bridget felt a sinking feeling in her stomach. She was so nervous. As they got out of the car she had mentioned to James her surprise to how far into the country his family lived. In fact, they owned 80 acres that surrounded their beautiful home. The Mackenvoy guys were rugged and very much into four wheelers and snow mobiles. As they walked up the long driveway Bridget could smell fall in the air even though it was still hot and humid outside. The trees hadn't started to change color just yet. Walking around the house she seen two long outdoor tables with a lot of food laid out. A big barn sat up on a hill in the background. All of the family was already sitting at the tables enjoying the food and talking. "I feel so nervous what if they don't like me?" She asked James with a trembling voice. "Just relax, sweetheart, you will be fine. I am sure they will love you," He said squeezing her sweaty hand tightly. Cullen noticed them walking up to the tables. "Hey, there they are. Thought you got lost!" He jokingly shouted. "Nope, we were just taking our sweet ass time," James said back to him with a smile. Bridget noticed a beautiful woman sitting at one end of the table and a man who looked very similar to James sitting at the other end. When he turned around to speak to James she could tell this was his dad. He had short straight blonde hair that was nicely trimmed with a small goatee and mustache. His build was identical to James even down to the shape of his eyes. Turning around in his seat he began to mumble with a cigar hanging out of his mouth, "It is about time, son. All the food is getting cold. So introduce us to this sweet little lady." He stood up to take her hand in his and shake it. His accent was very deep and his clothes spoke volumes as to how rich he was. James waited for his dad to sit back down when he began to introduce her, "Ok, this is Bridget everyone. This of course is my daddy, Colton. I will just start around the table from the right." Everyone began to laugh, except for the woman sitting at the end of the table. "You already know

Cullen, Marcus, Olivia. On the other side of the table here is my baby sister Emma and the grumpy looking guy you see there is Rick, Cullen's daddy." Rick looked over with a sour grimace on his face, "You want grumpy I will show you grumpy." James smiled and grabbed Bridget by the hand and walked her to the woman sitting at the far end of the table. "This is my momma, Victoria." Victoria stood up and looked her up and down. She slowly reached out to shake her hand. "It is a pleasure to meet you I am sure," She said in a stern voice. Bridget could feel a chill from her. Standing at an impressive 5 foot 8 inches she was a beautiful woman. Long Dark wavy hair with big dark doe eyes. Her eyelashes were long and beautiful along with her perfectly manicured eyebrows. Bridget couldn't get over her beauty and felt a little put off by her demeanor. Rick stood up to shake her hand and she couldn't absorb the sheer body of this man. He stood 6 foot 4 inches with a big chest and huge arm muscles. He had short wavy brown hair and brown eyes. His face was cleanly shaven and he had a pronounced cleft in his chin. Out of the corner of her eye she caught the tattoo on his left shoulder. It was of a huge snake with a big letter M behind it. Underneath the snake was simply the word Cobra. Bridget walked over to shake Emma's hand and she was very pleasant. Only being 5 foot 4 inches, Rick looked like a tower standing next to her. She was a spitting image of her mother. She had long dark wavy hair and those same big beautiful dark eyes. She had a sweet voice, not as high pitched as Olivia's. Bridget felt welcome by everyone, except Victoria. There was something not right about how she kept staring at her. Bridget felt as though she was a rodent that invaded their afternoon picnic. James and Bridget sat down in between Rick and Emma. Victoria asked a few questions to Bridget, but she didn't seem interested in the conversation as they were all sitting now eating their meal. All the sudden Victoria looked past Bridget and said excitedly, "Jackie, you made it!" James put his head down and rubbed it in aggravation. Bridget turned to look and there she was. The same beauty from Canada. Looking like her usual playboy model herself. Victoria walked over to greet her and even kissed her cheek. Emma turned to Bridget trying to reassure her not to feel bad, "This is just the way our momma is. She loves Jackie, please don't take it personally." Everyone else just sat at the table and continued to eat, pretending like nothing was out of place. Jackie came over and sat down in between Cullen and Olivia at the table. "So how is everyone? Hello again Bridget, it is nice to see you made it safely," Jackie said in a sarcastic manner. "Hi Jackie, and thank you," Bridget replied back kindly. Victoria spoke up, "Bridget was telling us all about your trip up north." Jackie looked over at Bridget with a sneer, "It could have went a lot better." Everyone could feel the tension role off of Jackie's tongue. James felt uneasy and jumped up from his seat, "Well everyone this has been nice, but I think it is time for us to go. Bridget is a little tired from the trip." Everyone kindly thanked Bridget for coming and reminded them they didn't need to rush off. But, James could tell how uncomfortable Bridget was feeling. He wanted everything to go perfectly, and now things were playing out as he had hoped. Grabbing Bridget by the hand they started to the car. "Your family is great James, thank you. But, your mom I think doesn't like me….. and Jackie?" Bridget said staring over at him. James shook his head before opening her car door, "I know…… I know they are like two peas in a pod. I am so sorry if that made you feel uncomfortable. Really it isn't as bad as it may seem. Just ignore some of their little antics." Bridget hopped in the car while James closed the door behind her. Sitting in the car on the drive back to her house, she wondered what kind of antics lay in store for her.

CHAPTER 8

The next morning as Bridget woke up to the sunny day her thoughts again returned to Jon and how he was doing. After all, he was one of her closest friends for such a long time. Reaching for her cell phone she realized it was 7:00am her time, Jon was in California so she would have to wait a little while. She got up to start her coffee and take her bath. After she finished dressing and getting her cup of coffee she heard a rap at her door. When she opened the door, Olivia and Cindy came walking in. "Hey there woman. If you are going to be a part of the Mackenvoy family you have got to get to know us gals!" Olivia said as she and Cindy walked into the house. "Great! I am looking forward to getting to know all of you," Bridget smiled back at Olivia. Suddenly, Olivia started to look a little pale in the face and asked where her bathroom was. She ran down the hall to the bathroom covering her mouth. Cindy and Bridget could hear Olivia vomiting after the door slammed shut behind her. "Poor girl. I hope her whole pregnancy isn't like this," Cindy said staring down the hallway. "Pregnancy?" Bridget asked quizzically. "Yes, she is pregnant and they just found out it is fraternal twins." Cindy said smiling back at her. "Wow! That is so exciting. They are getting married here in two weeks right?" Bridget asked Cindy while they heard the bathroom door open. "Oh my god I think I am dying. Whatever you girls do think twice about pregnancy. It isn't as beautiful as most people make it out to be," Olivia softly said laying back on the sofa. "Do you need anything?" Bridget asked standing up offering to get her anything she needed. "Yes some water, please," Olivia asked as she wiped the sweat off her forehead. "Damn, why can't this happen to the guys? I mean, we go through hell and all they have to worry about is getting a boner at an unsavory time and embarrass them." Olivia moaned while she continually wiped her face. Cindy and Bridget both giggled and agreed with her at the same time. Olivia explained to Bridget the whole situation how the pregnancy wasn't planned and it wasn't really a shotgun wedding. They had already planned their wedding the previous winter before she became pregnant. Marcus was thrilled to find out he was having twins, but also a little shocked. Olivia was happy, just very sick. The whole morning the girls got to know one another much better. Bridget mentioned wanting to call Jon to see how he was doing. Olivia explained to her that James would not be upset with her. He is a jealous type, but not controlling. As long as she doesn't give him a reason not to trust her, he will always respect her friends. Even if they are ex-boyfriends. Bridget dialed Jon's number and he picked up after two rings. "Hey Bridget, how are you doing?" He asked excitedly. "I am doing well, how are you settling in there in California?" Bridget asked him. "I am already all signed up for classes and I am extremely excited about this! But, there are a lot of talented people here and I have my work cut out for me!" He said laughing. "Listen Jon, I just thought I would warn you that I decided to move to Tennessee and see where things will go with James," Bridget explained as Jon's end remained quiet. "Jon, are you there?" She asked him as she looked at Olivia and Cindy. "Yes I am here, but I have to say I feel a little concerned about that kind of a drastic decision. Are you sure this is what you want I mean you don't even know the guy?" He said to her. "Well that is the whole point, I needed to move closer to him so we can get to know one another," Bridget continued to explain. Jon became a little frustrated and he said, "Whatever…… listen I have to go for now. But, I will definitely keep in touch. And I am very happy for you if this is what you want." Bridget let him know this is most certainly what she wanted before they said their goodbyes. After getting off the phone with Jon the girls talked about the wedding and babies until afternoon when Marcus called Olivia to ask where she was at. It was a wonderful day and Bridget felt like finally she was falling into place and this was feeling like her home. Just before Olivia started to go out the door she had some advice for her, "When it comes to Victoria just ignore her nit picking. She is a socialite and she don't really care about people's character. Don't let that sour you on James. He is a great man and I think you will be happy with him. I have thought of him as my own brother for a while now and I know him well. Just be patient with him." Bridget took her words to heart. She was going forward and jumping in with both feet. She adored James and every time she was around him her heart would beat so fast. She knew this was love. James showed up that evening after a long day working on his accounting degree. College had begun for Marcus, Cullen and James. James was going for a degree in Accounting while Cullen was concentrating on Business. They all had the same goal, to work for the family business. But, they also had their band to think about. They were already so talented and had written their own music, all they needed now was to get their sound out there. Colton and Rick weren't thrilled their sons were pursuing a music career, but as long as they finish school and make the family business their top priority they would leave them alone. All the girls were behind the guys all the way. However, they all three had a feeling of disgust thinking of all the women throwing themselves at their men. But, each of them wanted to be nothing but supportive. That night James and Bridget discussed the upcoming wedding and the pregnancy. Being with each other felt right. They began kissing and feeling excited for one another when James' phone rang. It was Jackie. Bridget realized if he was going to be ok with her and Jon, then she had to be ok with him and Jackie. But, she couldn't help but feel jealous. After all this woman was so much prettier and obviously his mother adored her. What did he see in her, then? After he hung up his phone he apologized and started to kiss her again. Bridget stopped kissing so she could talk to him, "James, what is it that you see in me? And be honest, no lies." James thought for a second while he looked into her eyes, "You are beautiful." With that sentence, Bridget rolled her eyes and scoffed. "Now stop it, listen to me. You are beautiful, smart, sexy, and there is something about your personality that just made me fall for you immediately. It is like I prayed for this certain type of woman to come into my life and there you were right in front of me. That silly dance you were doing when you tried to knock my block off just grabbed me right away," He said rubbing her cheek with his fingers. Bridget began laughing hysterically, "I can't believe I did that. There is a reason I don't dance or try to be funny in public. I am a clumsy person." James smiled and said, "All the more reason I adore you. You aren't afraid to be silly and you don't think makeup is an essential to survive. You can roll out of bed and just be the prettiest thing I have ever seen with sleep crust and all." They both laughed and she said, "Well that is always a plus then that you love my sleep crust, too. Thank you so much for explaining that to me. I feel a little better now." He looked at her a little confused, "So this is about Jackie? Honey, I told you things were over with her before I even fell for you. She and I just shouldn't have gotten together in the first place. Once again I was trying to make my momma happy, not myself. I won't lie, Jackie is extremely sexy and I did enjoy my time with her. But, you are the woman I have been dreaming about since I was 15. Someone who will knock me off my feet." Bridget didn't know what to say. She felt so good about what he was saying, but all at the same time she felt like maybe she couldn't be this person he was seeing. The way he described her made her feel perfect when she knew she wasn't. James spent the night with her and when morning came he had to leave early. Things seemed to be falling into place for her. She had her new friends now and best of all, she had James. That day she thought she would take a trip to the café where James said everyone seems to frequent. It was a cute little shop that sat right in the center of town. When she walked in she didn't see Cindy or Olivia, so she walked to the counter to order a coffee and grab a paper. After grabbing her coffee she stepped off to the side so other people could get what they needed. Looking around for the cream and sugar on the counter she could hear behind her a man talking to the cashier. He was being very flirtatious and Bridget couldn't help but grunt and roll her eyes when she heard what he was saying to the cashier. Of course, the girl behind the counter was eating it up. He heard Bridget make her noise and he swayed over her way. As she started to pour the sugar in her coffee a voice behind her startled her, "I haven't seen you around here before. I think I would have remembered it if I had." Bridget jumped spilling her sugar on the counter. She turned around to look at him. He was tall with dirty blonde hair that hung down into his eyes and around his ears. His eyes were a glassy blue and he had thick sexy eyebrows. "I can't believe some of those lines work," She said staring at him. "I am not exactly trying to pick her up," He whispered getting close to her face, "She just likes me so I flirt with her to make her feel good." Bridget rolled her eyes, "I see," She said turning around to finish adding the sugar to her coffee. "So do you take coffee with your sugar?" He asked seriously as he watched her pour in the packet of sugar. "Why is it your business? I may be new to town, but I am not looking for new friends or to be picked up so if you wouldn't mind to leave me alone, thanks." She grabbed her paper and coffee and walked over to a table by a window. He looked at the lady behind the counter and said, "Geesh, women these days. You would think if she was coming to our town she would be a little bit friendlier." The lady behind the counter smiled and flipped her hair over her shoulder. "You know I am friendly. If you ever want to go out you know where you can find me," The cashier said. He just smiled turned to look at Bridget for a moment and then back to the cashier. "I will see you later, Karen, thanks for being polite," He said once again turning to look at Bridget with a nasty sneer as he left the café. Karen looked at her with a shrug and walked to the back of the store. Bridget couldn't help but to feel a little out of her element at this moment. What a jerk she thought and a pig all at the same time. Just as she was thinking of leaving the café Cindy walked in. "Oh hey, how are you doing?" She said walking up to the table Bridget was at. "I am good thanks. Do you want to sit here with me?" Bridget asked. "Sure, let me get my coffee and I will be over," Cindy said as she walked back to the counter to order her coffee. When she got back to the table she sat down and started to talk, "I am so excited, Matt asked me to marry him last night!" Bridget screamed, "Oh really? I am so happy for you!" She grabbed her hand to see her ring. "I knew he was going to ask, it wasn't like it was a surprise. I am just thrilled. I love him so much and we have been together for about a year now." Just as she finished her sentence she made a nasty face and looked down at her coffee mumbling, "See that guy there that just came in?" Bridget turned to look. "Yeah, who is he?" Bridget looked curiously. "That is Joey Hillenbrand. Oh gross, and the guy getting ready to come in the door is Walker Hillenbrand his cousin. They are both major assholes. Just ignore them if they try to talk to you ok?" Cindy asked her in a serious manner. "Yeah, sure," She said turning her head again to get a glimpse of these horrible Hillenbrand men that she was told about the few days before. Both men had dirty blonde hair that they both wore kind of long. They were both very handsome. They didn't look like they would be trouble makers to Bridget. Walker glanced over at the girls table and they both hurried to turn their heads seeming uninterested. The men took their coffees and left without a word. "Ick, I can't stand them. They are always making trouble so if you see them around just walk the other way," Cindy warned her. Bridget watched the truck pull away out the window and shook her head wondering what could be so bad about these young men?

CHAPTER 9

The evening started out hot for a late September day. This was the day for Marcus and Olivia's wedding day! Olivia looked beautiful in her wedding dress, even with the cute little bump she was sporting. Marcus looked handsome as he usually did. There was still one person Bridget hadn't met yet. Before the ceremony a very kind lady with light brown hair and thin shaped brown eyes came over to Bridget and gave her a big hug. "Hello sweetheart, I am sorry I didn't get to meet you the other day," The lady said with a giggle as she squeezed Bridget in her arms. Bridget looked at her with confusion on her face. "Oh, gee I am sorry my name is Mare….. Mare Mackenvoy, Rick's wife," Mare said grabbing Bridget's hand to shake it after the hug. "Oh ok it is so nice to meet you finally! James mentioned you before, but I am sorry I totally forgot," Bridget said with a smile. "That is okay! I am just glad to finally meet you!" Mare said walking away. She seemed like a terrific lady and she obviously had a great sense of humor. Bridget noticed everyone sitting down to get ready for the ceremony while James stood at the altar with his brother. Olivia's father walked her down the aisle as is custom and everything went off without a hitch. No morning sickness interfered with this occasion. When James and Bridget arrived at the building the reception was being held at, she couldn't believe how beautiful everything was. She wasn't used to all the riches. The food was exquisite and it really looked like something out of a fairy tale. Olivia came over to talk to Bridget after they cut the cake. "Hey, how are you doing wasn't everything beautiful? I am Mrs. Marcus Mackenvoy, I am so excited!" Olivia was jumping and squeezing Bridget in her arms. "I am so happy for you both, Olivia. You definitely deserve this," Bridget said as Olivia gave a beautiful smile. "Are you going to dance?" Olivia teased Bridget. "No, I don't think so I am just not good at that and I don't want to make a fool of myself in front of all these rich people," She whispered to Olivia. "Yeah, well just wait until you have to go to all the Mackenvoy and Hillenbrand parties." Olivia said as two ladies kissed her cheek congratulating her. "Oh, what are those?" Bridget asked Olivia with that same look she gave James the first day they arrived in town. "They just have these ridiculous parties for Halloween, New Years, Valentines…. they are really just to prove one family is better than the other honestly. None of the public are allowed at these parties unless we invite them. They just throw them while each tries to show the other up is all," Olivia explained as Cindy came over to grab Olivia for the throwing of the Bouquet. Bridget looked around for James and seen him standing with Cullen and Matt by the bar. She walked over and whispered to him about the parties she didn't know about. James looked off in the air and bit his lip. "Oh yeah that. We can talk about it after the reception, babe. Those parties aren't a big deal and you don't even have to go so I didn't bring it up to you yet. But, if we ever get married those parties are par for the course," James said with a kiss on her cheek. She looked at him with an aggravated look as he began pushing her and said, "Go! You are going to miss the throwing of the bouquet." Bridget walked over where all the single ladies were standing. When Olivia threw the bouquet, Cindy was the one who reached out and caught it. Bridget didn't lunge for it since she felt she was too young to marry. Backing away from the crowd she didn't notice Victoria walk up behind her. When she turned around she was stunned by her presence so close to her. "Oh, I am sorry Mrs. Mackenvoy. I didn't see you there," Bridget said nervously using her hand to push her bangs out of her eyes. "I seen you," Victoria said giving a sly smile. "Olivia makes a beautiful bride and she will be a fantastic mother. Don't you agree?" Victoria asked as her eyes studied her. Bridget looked at Olivia and looked back at Victoria. "Yes, she is a fantastic girl," Bridget said smiling. "Some ladies are born regal and then some just don't have it," Victoria said with a small chuckle. She looked Bridget up and down once more before she walked away. Bridget felt the tension deeply at that moment. Victoria couldn't stand Bridget, and soon she would find out unwelcome she was to the Mackenvoy family. Nothing Bridget would ever be able to do could impress Victoria, no matter how hard she tried. Victoria's mind was already set in stone about her and she secretly wished James would break things off with Bridget. After the reception James and Bridget started back to her house. It was very late and Bridget was tired. James came up behind her helping her take her dress off and whispered, "Do you want me to stay the night?" She closed her eyes as James kissed her neck softly. She nodded her head yes as he wrapped his hands around her waist. She didn't tell him about the encounter with Victoria. But, she still couldn't help to feel like he was leaving her in the dark about a lot of things. James spun her around and began kissing her romantically as he took off her panties. This was the first night they made love with her mind on other things. However, Olivia and Marcus' honeymoon began perfect. They flew in to Miami around 1:00am. That didn't matter to either of them. Marcus carried her over the threshold into the hotel room and gingerly laid her down on the bed. Taking off his clothes as he stared at her. He whispered to her how happy he is that she is finally his wife. Removing her shirt he kissed her lower belly and glanced up to smile at her, "I think they are happy, too." Olivia giggled as he took off her panties. Kissing her inner thighs he made his way between her legs as she gasped feeling his soft tongue massage her. Trying to be gentle he slid inside her and made love to her gently for the next hour until they both collapsed in exhaustion. A month had passed after Marcus and Olivia's wedding and Bridget was falling into her new life quiet well. It was now October 31st and time for the first big party. This one didn't seem too bad for Bridget since everyone dressed up in costumes. It was not a formal kind of party so she felt comfortable. Walking into the same big building where Marcus and Olivia had their wedding reception a month earlier, Bridget felt excited to be a part of it. Dressed in a sexy devil costume, she looked around the dance floor to see who all was at the party. James wore a terminator costume which made her feel very turned on seeing his muscles sticking out of his tight shirt. Olivia was dressed in a kitten costume with the adorable baby bump poking out the front. There were so many other costumes she was getting a kick out of. She noticed the Mackenvoys stayed on one side of the gymnasium while the Hillenbrands stayed on the other. There was a balcony that overlooked the gym. All of the elders from both families sat up there like they were too good to be down near the dance floor. As Bridget looked around she couldn't help but feel a little out of place with all the rich folks. Jackie swayed over to Bridget and James' table they were sitting at. "Hey, James would you do me a favor and dance with me to this song I adore it?" She asked him with a sexy tone to her voice. James looked at Bridget hesitating. Jackie reached down and grabbed James' hand. "You don't mind do you?" She asked looking at Bridget as she pulled him onto the dance floor. Bridget felt aggravated, but didn't want to cause a scene so she walked to the punch table to get a drink. She tried to pretend not to notice that Jackie was occupying James' time on the dance floor. One thing she did seem to enjoy very much was the music that was played was all from the 80's and 90's time frame. In her opinion, they didn't make music like they used to. As she poured her drink a man came up behind her to get himself a drink as well. He was wearing a zorro mask and a black cape. "Well I will be," He said with a cheesy smile. Bridget looked up at him a little curious. Looking into his eyes through the mask she couldn't quiet pin it down where she seen him before. Then she noticed the blonde hair and sexy lips. "I know you remember me. Sugar with your coffee," He said rubbing his chin. She just stared for a moment at his face. "Oh, yeah I remember. You are a Hillenbrand?" She asked in a quizzical manner. He shook his head yes and gave her a wink. "That is correct. Why are you here? I am assuming you know someone from the other family or you wouldn't be here. You are not a friend of my family so who are you here with?" He asked looking around the dance floor. Bridget pointed in James' direction while holding her cup and said, "James Mackenvoy. We have been dating for a while." He looked at the floor laughing and then he glanced over at James. "Hmmmm, does he know that?" He asked looking back into her eyes. Bridget felt sad and looked down. "Well then I feel sorry for you. You could do so much better," He said sarcastically walking away. Cindy came jogging up to her as she watched him walk away. "James has been watching you two the whole time, what are you doing?" Cindy grumbled. "What do you mean what am I doing, I was getting a drink and this guy came over to talk to me," Bridget said taking another sip from her cup. "Are you crazy? That is the worst Hillenbrand of them all, besides Walker. His name is Billy and he is a huge whore dog, I mean terrible. He sleeps with some of the girls, but most of them he just gets them to give him head jobs. A real charmer let me tell you." Bridget listened as she kept looking at Billy across the room. "James really hates him. He is the brother to Joey and cousin to Walker. He is also the biggest trouble maker of the bunch. He is very intense, fights over the stupidest shit. If you know what is good for you don't fall for his charming friendly behavior. This is just great, now that he knows you are with James he will use it to make him crazy. Don't let him," Cindy said sternly pulling her by the arm to the table. James continued to watch Bridget as he and Jackie danced to "Your Still The One" By Shania Twain. This was the night Bridget would see how bad the fights could get. After the dance with Jackie, James didn't walk directly over to Bridget. He looked at her and then started over towards Billy without saying a word to her. "Hillenbrand!" James yelled. Billy turned around with a smile on his face. "Yes dear," Billy said to James. "Don't fuck with me!" James shouted as he pushed Billy. "Hey you mother fucker don't you put your hands on me!" Billy shouted back and then he began to laugh as he said, "You know everyone says I juggle women I would say you do your fair share. That cute little thing you are hanging with has a nice ass on her do you think I could have a test run?" James acted as though he was going to walk off shaking his head and smiling. Before everyone knew it, James sucker punched Billy in the jaw. The fight was intense as they punched each other in the face with force. Billy picked James up and threw him onto a table. The table shattered as Bridget screamed covering her eyes. Marcus and Cullen ran over to stop the fight, while Joey egged Billy on. Bridget was very upset at what she was seeing. She ran over begging them to stop. She didn't like seeing James fighting like this. Jackie ran over and yelled at Billy, "Stop hitting him you jerk!" Then Jackie looked at Bridget. "Are you happy this is what you wanted isn't it?" She asked Bridget nastily. "What…. I don't know what you are talking about, I said a few words to him that is it. I didn't start this," Bridget shouted at Jackie as Billy and James continued to fight. "Bullshit, and now Victoria and Colton have seen it too," Jackie said pointing up at the balcony. Bridget was confused as to what she was supposed to have done to cause this. After all, she didn't even know who Billy Hillenbrand was when he came up to talk to her. Colton pushed by Bridget while Rick walked calmly passed Jackie. As Bridget turned around she seen Colton and Rick walking up to grab a hold of James. Rick pushed Billy hard up against a wall. "Take your hands off my brother you son of a bitch!" Joey yelled as Rick held Billy up against the wall with his hand. He then turned around quickly still holding Billy with one hand while he pushed Joey away with his free hand. "Fuck off you little wimp,"

Rick grumbled. Colton grabbed James by the shirt and pulled him up off the floor. "James you fucking pussy, you are lucky your daddy pulled me off you," Billy laughed as Colton pushed James out the side door of the gym. Bridget looked at Billy rudely and ran off after James. When Bridget walked out into the hallway she seen Colton laying into James. "Just what the hell were you thinking, son? This is not the time and place to pull this shit," Colton said with his face a few inches from James'. "You know what he is up to, daddy, and I am not going to put up with it," James said out of breath with blood dripping from his mouth and nose. Bridget slowly walked up to James. "James," Bridget whispered rubbing his arm. "Why would you do that?" She asked in a trembling voice. "Why would you talk to him?" James asked her breathing heavily from the adrenaline. She looked at him for a moment in confusion. "I didn't know who he was I am sorry," She said turning around to look at Colton as well. James stood for a moment trying to catch his breath. Colton looked at her intensely. "Now you know who he is. Stay away from that dirt ball if you know what is good for you. He isn't nothing but a piece of trash," Colton said as he walked off to give them their privacy. Bridget started hugging James and began to cry. "I don't want you fighting like that, please don't do that," She said as she wrapped her arms around his neck and held him tightly against her. She ran her hands through his hair as she kissed his cheek. "I'm sorry but, I had to show him he can't walk all over me and flirt with my girl. Babe, you just don't know him," James said. She thought for a moment and said, "But, he didn't come on to me, he was just talking to me." James interrupted her and said, "That is how it starts with him, always. He don't care about any woman. He has one goal, to get laid or in this case to fuck me over and I will not let him do it." Bridget grabbed James' face so she could look him in the eyes. "I love you, you don't have to worry about that with me. I am a loyal person and I only have eyes for you. I am yours and he will not have any impact on me no matter what he does, okay?" She said looking him deeply in the eyes. James shook his head and wiped his face with his hand. In the gym, people were picking up the aftermath of their scuffle. Jackie stared at Billy and shook her head. "You are such a shit, Billy Hillenbrand," She said as she picked up pieces of the broken table. "Come on prom queen, you know if I showed any interest in you then those legs would be wrapped around me so quick," Billy said ogling her. Jackie laughed and rolled her eyes. "In your dreams rodeo boy," She said as she walked off. The party broke up and Victoria stood angrily, staring down at Billy Hillenbrand from the balcony in disgust. This family was like stray dogs to her. Billy's dad, Packard, stood on the opposite side of the balcony staring at Victoria with a smirk. Victoria glanced at Packard and walked down the stairs and exited the gym.

CHAPTER 10

The next day Bridget thought about the night before. She was disgusted with what she saw. She reached to grab her phone to call Jon. The phone rang several times with no answer. Sitting her phone down, she felt a sudden urge of sadness come over her. The phone rang and she quickly grabbed it to see if it was Jon, it was James. She stared at the phone for a second and didn't answer. Suddenly, there was a knock at the door. When she opened the door she was surprised to find Victoria standing there. "May I come in? Thank you," She said as she pushed by Bridget. Looking around the small house she turned to Bridget. "This is quaint. Is my son keeping you up to your liking I am assuming?" She asked her in a stern voice. Bridget noticed that as she spoke to her and looked around her home she was stiff. No emotion at all. She didn't seem kind to her as she did Jackie. "Yes, but I will get me a job and pay the rent for this place I just haven't had time," Bridget began to explain. Victoria made a small attempt to smile. "Nonsense, why work when you have all the help you need? I am not going to mince words. My son is very important to me. Our family are respectful demur people. I don't appreciate the silliness that went on last night," Victoria said as she walked up to her. Bridget stared down at the floor. Not knowing what to say or how to talk to her. Victoria grabbed Bridget's chin to make her look up at her as she began to feel aggravated. "If you are going to date my son, you are going to act more like a lady and less like….. what you are. If you do anything to embarrass this family you will pay for it. I promise you that," She said and then letting go of her face she started toward the door, "I will let myself out. You remember what I said, my dear." After Victoria left the house Bridget sat down and tried to collect herself. She was very upset. What was she going to do? This was much more than she bargained for. And she didn't even know what she had done wrong the night before. What Bridget didn't realize is Victoria meant her threats. Noticing James had left her a message, she decided to call him back. He immediately began apologizing for what had happened the night before. She didn't tell him about the visit from his mother. Bridget decided she wouldn't go to the coffee shop anymore without Cindy or Olivia out of fear of running into Billy and being accused of wrong doing. Jon never found the time to call her back, but she realized he was busy with his own life. She couldn't help but feel abandoned with no friends at this moment. It was now November and Thanksgiving was coming up fast. The cold winters were always hard on Bridget. She suffered from some depression around that time and it was difficult to see the light at times. This year she was terrified as to how she could handle this winter. She was in a new town, around different kinds of people, her true friends were far away from her, and the man she loved she was still getting to know. James invited Bridget to the Thanksgiving dinner at the Mackenvoy manor. She didn't want to go, but she knew if she didn't that would be a smack in the face to James. The day had arrived for the big Thanksgiving dinner, she agreed to go to. James picked her up at 4:00pm sharp. When they pulled up to the mansion Bridget could feel the nausea in the back of her throat. Being in a relationship shouldn't be this hard she thought. Walking into the dining area her mouth was so dry. It felt like she had cotton shoved clear back to her uvula. Already sitting at the table was Rick, Mare, Cullen, Olivia, Marcus, Colton, Victoria and Emma. Mare was the first to welcome Bridget to the dinner table. She was very kind and Victoria took a long sip of her wine pretending Bridget wasn't even there. Everyone sat and talked over dinner for the next hour. Olivia's pregnancy was progressing well. They found out they were having a boy and a girl. Everyone was ecstatic. While Cullen teased Emma, James stood up from his seat and left the room. All the sudden Emma let out an "Oh my god". Bridget, Olivia and Marcus turned around to see what the fuss was about. James was on one knee holding up a gorgeous diamond ring. "Bridget, I know this isn't extremely romantic. But I wanted to ask you in front of my family if you would be my wife?" Bridget was so surprised. She said yes before she knew it and wrapped her arms around James' neck and kissed him. Everyone at the table congratulated them, except Victoria. She stared at James and Bridget being overly affectionate and she looked as though she was about to lose her dinner. Olivia was screaming with excitement. She adored Bridget and felt as though they were the perfect couple. It's true she never got along too well with Jackie. Her personality seemed to suit Bridget and Cindy's much better. The girls could be silly and not have to be so serious all the time. Status wasn't important to Olivia as it was to Jackie. The winter was rough, cold and snowy. Bridget felt depressed, but she was still happy all at the same time. She had James and that was good enough. Victoria wasn't the most pleasant to be around that winter. She made it plain to Colton that she didn't think their son should be marrying a girl of limited means. But, Colton really didn't care as long as his son was happy. And James was very happy. There was another fight between Billy and Marcus during that winter. Nobody knows what it was over. It was surely the Hillenbrands being their normal selves. The second party Bridget went to was the New Year's Eve party. The building was decorated in beautiful white lights everywhere. There wouldn't be a fight at this dance. But, James would get his way and dance with his fiancée. She usually didn't do this. She was too self- conscious to let herself go. Especially around all the rich people. She could feel it, 2001 was going to be a good year for her. There was a beautiful balcony that was outside of the gym passed the bar. Bridget took a walk out onto the balcony and looked out at the cold snow covered lawn. "It is a nice night isn't?" A voice said behind her. When she turned around she seen Billy Hillenbrand in his black tie suit. "It could be better, I hate the cold," Bridget said stiffly looking back over the balcony. "Would you like to dance," Billy snuck up and whispered in her ear. She turned around and said, "I don't want to dance and I would appreciate it if you go back into the party. I am waiting for my fiancée and if he catches us talking I am sure he will be upset." Bridget turned back around ignoring Billy, hoping he would leave. She waited for a minute and relaxed when she assumed he left. "You know just because you are marrying a Mackenvoy, doesn't mean you have to be nasty towards me," Billy whispered again in her ear. Suddenly, Bridget heard James shout, "You never learn do you?" She turned around quickly and Billy began to laugh, "I don't take orders from the likes of you. She isn't married yet she can talk to anyone she wants to." James started to stomp up to Billy, but Bridget intervened. "Please James don't, I can handle it just fine," She said looking at his angry face. Billy walked by them smirking as he passed them. James stared at Bridget letting out a loud breath. "Calm down, he isn't anyone to me. You completely have my heart," Bridget said kissing James softly. The rest of January went slowly as it usually does for Bridget. That February, Olivia gave birth to two healthy babies. Olivia didn't handle pain well. During the entire labor process she screamed at the top of her lungs in that high pretty voice of hers, although it didn't sound all that pretty during this instance. They named the twins Justin and Amanda. Marcus was overly thrilled with the birth of his kids. Life was on the fast track for them, but that was ok. He would have his degree soon and he would be taking his bar exams. Bridget was busy planning her wedding for the following summer. Since summer was her favorite season she set the date for June 21, 2001. It seemed special to her in a way.

She didn't want a huge wedding, which was fine with Victoria. She felt ashamed that her son was marrying someone of limited means. That spring James invited Bridget's parents and siblings to the mansion to get to know everyone. The trip for the Case's was very uncomfortable. They could feel the disgust coming from Victoria, but everyone else in the family seemed pleasant. Colton and Rick had a way to them though that made Bridget's dad uneasy. He felt like they were much harder shelled then they let on. Bridget's parents didn't feel comfortable with Victoria at all. They felt like there was something evil about her. Mare was the only one who made everyone feel at home. Cullen's mom was a fantastic character. She never judged anyone and made you feel like you were just as good as she was. It was funny to see her littleness compared to big ole Rick. It seemed like an odd match, but it just fit perfectly. Rick was cunning and Mare was just as smart. So it was no wonder Cullen turned out to be exceptionally bright and strong. When he would fight, he would almost always win. Nobody much cared to start anything with Cullen Mackenvoy. He had a muscular chest and rock hard arms. He was so strong, but yet a silly teddy bear all at the same time. Nonetheless, Patty was so happy for her daughter's upcoming wedding she helped her plan it out. The spring came and went with nothing special happening with either family. And before she knew it, it was finally June! Bridget's attitude was so much happier. Her nerves were starting to get to her. During her final fitting for her wedding dress Jackie made a surprise visit. She walked in swaying side to side, eyeing Bridget up and down. "Don't you look beautiful?" She said. Bridget turned around to thank her. "I have to admit I was surprised by your engagement," Jackie mustered under her breath. "Jackie don't start please," Olivia pleaded. Bridget stopped Olivia, "No it is okay Olivia. Whatever do you mean Jackie?" Bridget asked while Jackie rolled her eyes and said, "Don't you find it odd how quickly James proposed to you? I mean, not long after the fight on Halloween with Billy, he asks you to marry him. Don't you ever wonder if maybe he is doing it out of not wanting to lose?" Bridget stared at Jackie for a moment. "What do you mean, he don't want to lose?" Bridget said feeling anxious. "Well, James and I had been together for a while and we talked about marriage ourselves we just never actually jumped into it. We knew we were too young. But, I never would leave him, he knew this. I would wait for him as long as he needed to and I would never have eyes for another man. You however, are the type that when things get tough….. you run. You aren't strong enough to be a Mackenvoy. And maybe he is just worried that Billy could get into your pants." Bridget started to get upset, "So what are you trying to say you think he is marrying me out of spite?" Bridget asked as she pulled the dress up over her head. "Maybe, maybe not but it has to make you wonder," Jackie teased. "I know James loves me, Jackie. This isn't a Fred Flintstone moment with him where he thinks he has to marry me to show he is the best. If you can't handle this then stay away from my wedding. You are only invited because Victoria adores you and you are still James' friend," Bridget snapped at her. Jackie laughed, "This marriage will fail. You will see." As she left the bridal shop, she turned flipping her hair off of her left shoulder blade to reveal a sexy tattoo that said "James". Bridget felt a little rattled by the encounter. Jackie did what she set out to accomplish. She put doubt in Bridget's mind. Olivia's babies were going on four months old when Cindy found out she too was now expecting. Matt was over the moon. He enjoyed spending time with Marcus' babies and couldn't wait to have one of his own. Cindy could swear he planned this, although she was just as happy about the pregnancy. She didn't have the morning sickness that plagued Olivia. James told Matt he needed to marry her to make it a proper family. Matt and Cindy would plan their wedding for the end of June. It wouldn't be a huge wedding. On June 21st, it was finally the wedding day and Bridget was so nervous. She had invited Jon, but he didn't show up. She felt a little crushed, but she understood. She was about to become Mrs. James Mackenvoy! Her family had made it for the wedding which made her very happy. Even Cullen had a new beauty on his arm. She was gorgeous with long straight brown hair and light brown eyes. Her name was Giselle and she was from Brazil. The wedding went off without a hitch. It was in a huge church and the reception was held at the same venue as Olivia and Marcus'. Bridget was walked down the aisle by her father, Robert. As she came closer to the altar, James' eyes began to well up as he looked at her in that beautiful dress. Bridget felt so nervous walking up to face James. She looked deep into his beautiful brown eyes as the minister recited the wedding vows. The whole time Bridget felt as though she was going to faint from the excitement and nerves! Cullen and Marcus stood behind James smiling with happiness. They adored Bridget and knew this was the right move for James. Victoria was appalled, there was nothing she could do to deter James now from marrying that girl of limited means. After the wedding Colton came over to kiss Bridget on the cheek. "Welcome to the family, darling," He said with his deep Texan accent. After the lovely dinner, James and Bridget cut their beautiful wedding cake. Bridget did her best not to smash the cake in his face, they still had their first dance together and she didn't want to ruin his suit. After the cutting of the cake, James and Bridget walked to the dance floor. The song "Silver Springs" By Fleetwood Mac. After their slow dance, the song "Hold On" By En Vogue began to play as everyone else began to dance. Before Bridget knew it, it was time to throw the bouquet. After Bridget threw the bouquet, Bridget's sister Sophia caught it happily. James walked up and whispered in Bridget's ear, "I can't wait to take you for our honeymoon." The wedding and reception was over by 2:00pm so they could catch their flight. They didn't plan on an extravagant honeymoon. He took her to Hawaii, where she had always wanted to go. The state was gorgeous and the wedding night was amazing. They had rented a little bungalow near the ocean coast. After a candle lit dinner by the ocean, he took her back to the bungalow. Bridget immediately went to the restroom and James waited for a while. He wondered what she could be doing that would take so long. His anticipation was growing wildly. She opened the bathroom door to reveal what she was wearing. His eyes looked her up and down to see a black lace mesh bra and g-string with stockings. He swallowed hard when he looked at her. She was so sexy to him, he couldn't wait to be with her as husband and wife. "Oh baby, you are so sexy. Now come here so I can touch you," He said to her. She smiled as she began to tease him with her movements. She felt a little shy in doing so. She didn't have much confidence in herself, but that didn't matter to him. He loved what he saw. He couldn't control himself, he felt as though he would go insane if he couldn't touch her. "Damn Bridget, you have to come here now I can't take it anymore. I have to make love to you now," He said raising up on the bed. "Patience my love," She said as she laid him down on the bed and took him in her mouth. She teased him with her tongue, it felt so erotic to him since she had all the control at the moment. She slid herself up onto his stomach, rubbing her wetness all the way up his chest. Finally, making her way to his face. She hovered above him for a moment. "Are you sure you want me?" She asked. He grabbed her hips pulling her down to his face. She gently sat down on his face, as he moved her panties off to the side so he could taste her. She gently rocked back and forth on his face. She could feel the intense orgasm as she let herself release into his mouth. He raised up and laid her on her back. He stopped for a moment and looked into her eyes. "Will you give me a baby and make me a daddy? I know it is a lot to ask so early on…." Bridget interrupted him, "I stopped taking my birth control awhile back I have been using a diaphragm, which I am not using at the moment." James smiled when he realized she had the same idea as he had all along. He gently slid himself inside of her, making passionate love to her. He was having trouble controlling his orgasm as she whispered in his ear how much she loved him. She screamed out from the sheer largeness of him as he pumped harder and faster. He couldn't hold back any longer as he could feel himself climax sending chills throughout his body. After they were finished making love, they realized they would be connected forever.

CHAPTER 11

The honeymoon was beautiful. James took her to the top of a hill for a picnic where they witnessed a small volcano eruption off in the distance. Everything felt so perfect. Bridget really didn't want to discuss Jackie on their honeymoon, but she couldn't help but bring up the tattoo. "James, can we talk about Jackie?" Bridget asked. "Do we have to honey? I mean this is our honeymoon I really don't want to think about her, my mother or the Hillenbrands," He said a little frustrated. "But, she has a tattoo with your name on her back shoulder. You don't think that is a little psychotic?" Bridget asked seriously. "It is a little strange, but I don't care what she does with her body. All I care about is you and I want you to feel safe and secure in our marriage more than anything," He told her rubbing her face. "But, she obviously thinks the two of you will be together or else she wouldn't have gotten it," Bridget said as James reached up and put his finger to her lips. "Don't think about Jackie, please. I know she does these things and she can be a little overwhelming, but I don't love Jackie. I told you already I never loved her the way a man should love a woman. Her tattoo is insignificant to me. If she wanted to alter her body in that way, that is her choice," He said taking a drink of his wine. "I noticed you all have a tattoo thing going." Bridget giggled. "Yes we do love our tattoos. We all will get one sooner or later on the arm, shoulder, back or chest," He said putting a grape into his mouth. "Or the private area," Bridget joked. James stopped chewing for a moment staring at her. "You are messed up…… I like it," He said smiling as he went in to kiss her. The rest of the honeymoon was just as wonderful as that night. But, all good things must come to an end and it was time to head back to normal life. When they arrived back in Tennessee it was back to usual, sort of. James had surprised Bridget with their new house. It was a modest beautiful two story home that sat out in the country only five miles from town. It had a complete basement for the band to do their practices. It also came with 20 acres of privacy. There was a small one bedroom guest house that sat behind the house, which James and Bridget were sure to christen. The stairs were off to the left as soon as you walked in the front door. The living room was off to the right. The kitchen was at the end of the hallway from the front door. There was an extra staircase passed the kitchen and laundry room that went up to the second floor where all the bedrooms were located. Bridget was so excited, her life was finally beginning with the man she adored. At the end of June Cindy and Matt married. Cindy's pregnancy wasn't too bad at all she was feeling great. On the fourth of July both families had their usual picnics at the park. This was the first time Bridget was seeing Billy and the other Hillenbrands since the Valentine's Day dance. James had left that morning to run some errands and he would meet Bridget at the park. While sitting at her picnic table Bridget stared at the Hillenbrand matriarch of the family, Packard. She could tell he was a hard man around the edges. He sat under the shade of a tree while he smoked his cigarette. He had short dark blonde hair that sat right above his ears and a goatee. His brother, Jack, looked similar in nature only shorter. Packard was 6 foot 2 inches, but Jack was only 6 foot even. He was known as a nut job around town. You didn't want to mess with Jack.

He loved his guns very much and shooting, as was Billy. They both would attend the annual gun contests every year in different towns. Billy was a bulls-eye shot with any gun. He never had to use the sights on his gun he just knew where the target was. Their main business was architecture, but they were deep into the horse business. Joey and Billy did most of the horse training around the area. If anyone needed a horse broke, they brought them to the Hillenbrand farm. All of the Hillenbrand men had either dirty blonde or dark blonde hair with blue eyes. The only exception at this time was Lisa, Packard's wife, and their daughter Monica. Monica and Lisa both had blonde hair, but they had green eyes. The Hillenbrand family looked so much different from the Mackenvoy family. Not only in hair or eye color, but in the way they dressed. Even though they were rich, their clothing was just like everyone else's. They didn't like to show off their pride with expensive clothing. Both families weren't involved in any type of illegal drugs, however drinking alcohol was the mainstay of their lives. James finally showed up to the picnic sporting a huge white patch on his left arm. Rick was the first to notice and said, "Hey dip shit let us see the ink. What did you get?" Cullen reached over to pull off his gauze and James smacked his hand away. Bridget sat and looked at him in surprise. "Alright, give me a minute here," He said looking over at Bridget as he pulled off the bandage and showed everyone the amazing artwork. It was a skull head with roses and barbed wire with Bridget spelled above the tattoo. Bridget sat down her soda she was drinking in shock. "Why did you do that?" She asked him while she softly touched it. "I wanted to put your name on my arm, you aren't mad are you?" She stared at the tattoo in amazement. "I am not mad, I am flattered in fact. I just hope that it won't doom us," She said with an ominous look. "Oh, come on that is superstitious nonsense," Olivia said rolling her eyes. James gave out a small laugh as Jackie stood up and walked away. Victoria looked at James with a nasty pinched face. Bridget looked at Victoria for moment then looked back at James with a huge smile on her face. Walker was looking across the lawn eyeing the whole scene. "Hey dickhead, our tattoos are much better than that is!" Walker yelled. Everyone ignored him while Bridget smiled and kissed James saying, "I do love it, thank you that is the sweetest thing anyone has ever done for me." After the fireworks James told Bridget he had something he needed to tell her and he was all excited, "Listen, I have some great news. The guys and I sent in our first round of music to a record label and we are hoping it gets picked up." Bridget was really excited for him, but also very scared. "Really, that is amazing baby I am so happy for you!" She said as she threw her arms around his neck. She wondered how Olivia, Cindy and Giselle felt about it. She knew Cindy wouldn't be happy. She didn't know Giselle well enough to guess how she would react. Giselle was a photographer in Brazil and came to the states for Cullen. Everyone knew the band would do so well. Their sound was similar to the Alice in Chains of the 90's. Close to the end of July, Cindy was going on her fourth month of pregnancy. Bridget was shopping at the local grocery store when Billy walked up behind her and said, "Hey stranger how are you?" When she realized who it was she turned back around without saying a word to him. "That's it be a stuck up bitch, see if I care," He said as he walked on past her. She watched him walk away when all the sudden she felt very sick to her stomach. She knew she was going to vomit any minute. She rushed to the bathroom and made it just in time. After being sick, she splashed her face with water. Resuming her quick shopping she grabbed a pregnancy test and headed home. She called up Cindy and Olivia to come over while she took the test. Cindy showed up first. "Hey there so you are feeling sick huh?" Cindy asked rubbing Bridget's forehead. Bridget nodded while she let out a long sigh. "Well take the test!" Cindy yelled. "I will I want to wait for Olivia," Bridget said in a tired sounding voice. Finally after twenty minutes Olivia showed up trying to pack in the twins in each arm and a diaper bag over her shoulder. "Oh my god, this sucks when Marcus is busy doing his thing," Olivia grumbled as she sat the babies down on the floor. All the guys were out of town for the day to promote their music, but they would be back the next day. "Ok, let's get this started!" Cindy excitedly said. "Ok, I am sure it is positive because I am still feeling sick," Bridget said as she walked off to the bathroom. "Well if it is you better hope it's not twins they are a handful!" Olivia shouted behind her. Then she looked at Cindy and smiled. Olivia and Marcus' babies looked just like him with the dark eyes and dark hair. They were definitely Mackenvoy through and through. Bridget came walking back into the room and sat the pregnancy test upside down on the living room table. "I am so nervous. I am only 19 years old and I am going to be a mom. I know this is positive I just feel so different lately. Last night while James was away I cried over a Golden Girls episode," She said as both Cindy and Olivia laughed. "Ok I can't take it anymore!" Bridget screamed grabbing the test. She screamed loudly and started laughing, "Look, it is positive!" All the girls screamed and hugged each other while the twins stared at them in terror. All the sudden Bridget stopped hugging and said, "Oh shit! You don't think it is twins do you? I would like one right now I don't know if I can handle two." Bridget eyes filled with terror. "Honey, you will be ok twins or not," Cindy said laughing still. "I can't wait to tell James," She said reaching for the phone. Olivia shouted, "NO! Don't tell him that way! You have to do this in person. Trust me his reaction will be hilarious. When Marcus found out we were having twins he fainted in the doctor's office." The girls laughed again and chatted for the next two hours about names and babies. Then Bridget's cell phone rang. "I bet that is my hubby," She said as she grabbed the phone and stared at it for a moment. "Well who is it?" Cindy asked. "It's Jon," Bridget said a little surprised. "Well answer it," Olivia pushed. "Hello Jon, it has been awhile," Bridget answered talking to him for a while. She told him how beautiful her wedding was and how she was soon to be a mom. He was quiet on the other end for a few seconds and then congratulated her. He himself was seeing someone also. Bridget felt very happy for him. She was also happy to know he landed his first acting role. She knew he would go far. Jon was a very talented sexy man. The next morning when James arrived home he rushed in the door happy to see his wife. "Babe, where are you? Babe!" He shouted as he looked around, but he didn't see her anywhere. Then she came down the stairs trying to hide her smile. He turned around to see her smiling at him. "Hey, I missed you baby," He said grabbing her up in his arms and spinning her around. "Ugh, please don't do that sweetie," She said while he excitedly told her about the record deal they made with a big company. He was so excited he was talking so fast she could barely keep up with him. When he finally calmed down he asked her how she was those few days without him. "I have something to tell you," She said staring deep into his eyes. "Oh yeah, what's that my angel," He asked as Bridget walked over and took out the pregnancy test she hid in the end table. She came walking up to him and said, "Close your eyes and hold out your hand." He started to close both eyes but started peeking with one. "Hey I said both eyes," She said with a giggle. She grabbed his hand and laid the test in his palm. He opened his eyes and looked down at the test. He looked up at her quickly and asked if that is what he thought it was. She smiled with tears in her eyes and said, "Yes." He grabbed her up again and spun her around. "Oh James you have to quit doing that," She said feeling very sick to her stomach. "Oh shit I am sorry are you really sick? Do you need anything? I will do whatever you need me to," He said excitedly. "No I am fine," She said while he grabbed his phone. "I have to call daddy, Marcus, Cullen… did you tell your family yet?" He asked with his mouth moving so fast she could barely understand him. "Yes, I did last night. They are happy for us," She said doing a little belch under her breath. James gave her a big kiss on the cheek and then called everyone he needed to call excitedly. Bridget felt nauseous and snuck off to the bathroom to vomit again. After James finished his calls he noticed her looking pale and had her lie down on the bed while he took care of her. He was very attentive and the best husband he could be for her. That

September James started his second year of Accounting and Marcus was finishing up law school. Cullen had finished his business degree already. Cullen also completed his Italian and Spanish language courses. He would get a kick out of speaking in Italian or Spanish when someone asked him something. Nobody would know what he would say to them. He and Giselle were getting very serious as well so he was having a great year. The guys found out there first album would be released soon and they would possibly have to tour in 2002. But, as of right now Bridget wasn't going to think about that. She was so happy with the baby being on the way and her house with her wonderful husband. Of course, she still had to deal with Victoria's nasty attitude about the whole thing. She did amazingly well dealing with it the best she could. In December they found out they were having a little girl. Cindy was wanting to be surprised by what she and Matt would have. For Christmas James wanted to get Bridget a pet. He brought home an adult Rottweiler/Pitt Bull mix he had adopted from an animal shelter. He wasn't in very good health, but James and Bridget wanted to care for him for his final few years he had left. They named him Dallas.

CHAPTER 12

Emma Mackenvoy was now 18 years old and so ready for the world. She had her sights set on veterinarian school. She was so beautiful, looking exactly like her mother. But, she didn't have the same demeanor as Victoria. She didn't have a mean bone in her body and she certainly didn't like the fighting either that went on with her brothers and the Hillenbrand men. She was always the first to offer babysitting duty to give Marcus and Olivia a break. She intended to do the same for James' little girl when she arrived. The due date of their little girl was coming up fast. It was now March 2002 and Bridget awoke to labor pains on this foggy rainy morning. She just assumed it was Braxton- hicks contractions so she didn't immediately tell anyone or rush to the hospital. A few hours later she was walking Dallas when the pain was too powerful to ignore. When she came in the front door she could hear the band practicing down in the basement. Walking down the hall holding her belly, she barely made it to the basement entryway when she interrupted the band. All the guys stood for a moment in shock and then everyone jumped into action. Eight hours later in the hospital Bridget was pushing to the best of her ability. She handled the labor well, but not without help of an epidural. James held her hand as she pushed and brought their little girl into the world. James cried when he held his little girl for the first time. They named her Megan. Matt couldn't help but get excited knowing his baby would be here soon too. He swore they were having a little boy so he was prepared. Everyone held the baby, but Victoria seemed cold even still with the birth of her new granddaughter. Bridget watched how Victoria held Megan. She was looking at her in a way that made Bridget feel uneasy. Jackie did not show up for the birth of their daughter. Not that it bothered Bridget, she was happy to not have to see her face during this wonderful time in her life. The next two months passed and Bridget fell into motherhood with grace. It seemed to come naturally to her even though she was still considered young to be married and have a daughter already. Cindy had also had her baby, a little girl. Even though Matt swore he was having a boy, it turned out he was going to have a little girl as well. They named her Shaina. The Hillenbrand family was growing as well. Monica, older sister to Joey and Billy, had a baby that prior year. A boy named J.T, short for Joshua Thayne. Monica was married to a man named Rusty. Packard was feeling a little uneasy with all the births that was happening with the Mackenvoys. This was a major thorn in his side. He needed to make sure his family was to prosper. So far it seemed as though the Mackenvoys were multiplying faster than fleas. That spring everyone received some annoying news when Colton and Packard sat both of their families down to tell them what the next four years had in store for them. Signing up with a cable network, both families were to have their lives put on air for the world to see. The money that would generate from the ratings would go directly to the charities each family had chosen. Now that James and his band's CD dropped it was a major hit and sent them to being number one for the year. Their band was named Hangman's Noose and they were the new "it" band. America was dying to tune in to see how these two families lived since rock stars were involved. Bridget was not happy about this at all. She was a very private person and didn't want the world to see the most private part of their lives. Since it was a cable network, nothing would be edited out of what was caught on camera. This made Victoria very nervous. Mostly because of Bridget. She didn't want her family to be made out to be the laughing stock of America. Bridget was the type that wouldn't hold her tongue to make others happy. To Victoria she wasn't very lady like. Bridget didn't want to have someone constantly watching over her to make sure she wouldn't do anything to embarrass the family. Victoria was like a never ending gnat that fluttered around your head. No matter how much you swatted at it, it never went away. Life was about to get really complicated for everyone. Olivia was not thrilled either about the whole reality show. It was hard enough dealing with life all on its own let alone someone filming in your face so many hours of the day. Olivia, Bridget, Cindy and Giselle all met at a local restaurant to have some food and talk. The guys were watching the kids for a change. The girls started to discuss what horrific tests would lie ahead for their marriages. Cindy started off complaining about how soon they will never even get to see their husbands because of the cd. "I know we won't get to see them much, Cindy, but we have to be supportive. They are our husbands we knew what they were wanting out of life before we married them," Olivia said taking a bite of her food. "I know, but didn't you guys secretly wish they wouldn't get discovered?" Cindy asked frustrated. "I will admit I kind of did," Bridget said slowly, "My reasons though are more of the jealous and selfish nature. I don't want other woman or even men ogling my husband and wanting in his pants. I mean, I know I am not the best looking in the world so what if those hot bimbos who look like Jackie steal him away. Oops I am sorry, Giselle, no offense you are gorgeous," Bridget smiled looking at Giselle. Everyone laughed as Giselle spoke up, "No, it is ok and I completely agree. It doesn't matter how beautiful one is you still can become jealous. Well look at it this way, Jackie is model material and she couldn't keep James' attention. Obviously, he isn't a shallow man and there is something about you that keeps him interested." Giselle had a point Bridget knew, but she still couldn't put away her insecurities. She knew now she would have to worry about a million Jackies out there. Olivia was a jealous type too. When she would get pissed people would listen because she would yell at the top of her lungs and cuss like a truck driver. Olivia also had a dirty side to her. She may have seemed mousy to everyone else, but in the bedroom she was a sex kitten. All the girls loved to tease her about it, but she didn't want this coming out on the show at all. She and Marcus had a habit of using sex toys and fetish type of articles during sex. "I am just so not looking forward to Mathew going away for a couple of months at a time. I just had Shaina he should be here with us. Not traveling the world doing shows," Cindy said dropping her fork and pushing her plate to the side. Bridget looked over at Cindy. "Hey, it will be ok. You know this right? We will all get through this and hopefully these tours won't happen too often," Bridget said trying to reassure Cindy. "Yeah, I will believe that when I see it," Giselle sarcastically said as she looked at her watch. "Uh, listen ladies I need to go. I will call you all sometime later this week," She said as she jumped up and rushed off. "God I hate her body," Olivia said checking out Giselle's ass as she walked away. "I am so envious of her face and body I would kill for that," Olivia still continued to envy her as she walked away. That summer the taping for the show began. Everyone was disgusted by it, even Colton and Packard, but they knew any type of publicity for charity was good. Sex while filming wasn't so easy for everyone. They had to sneak to do it because it seemed as though there was a camera in every room following them. In July when Megan was four months old and Olivia's twins were a year and a half old, Hangman's Noose took off for their first tour. It was only going to be for a few months around parts of the U.S, but the girls were upset. They knew this was coming. It was so hard watching their husbands leave them. Especially having to take care of the kids all on their own. Marcus had already passed his bar exams, but he figured he would open his office that autumn after the tour. James was to start his job with his father's company doing the books and Cullen was employed there as well. Bridget couldn't help but feel as though it was too much too fast. She not only had Megan to take care of, but she also had Dallas to tend to. She had an idea to help out with the distance while James was on the road. The first two days while he was on tour Bridget didn't talk to him much on the phone. He and the band were so busy. She felt a little neglected, not to mention having to keep Cindy calmed down. Cindy thought she was going to lose her mind without Matt. She would call his cell phone constantly, when she wouldn't get an answer her mind would jump to conclusions. Olivia would just sit around and cry at times missing Marcus. Being on the phone with him wasn't near as good as holding him in her arms. She felt empty while he was gone. The twins were getting into everything all the time. Finally, James called Bridget one night around 8:00pm, she had just gotten Megan to bed. "I miss you, James, so much. How long do you think you will be gone for?" Bridget asked him. "I am hoping we will be back in a few weeks. Is everything going okay there, is Megan doing alright? James asked her sadly. "She is doing okay, she misses her daddy," Bridget said with a sad voice. James made a small weepy sound and uttered, "I miss her too, I am so sorry I am not there. I am so torn about this whole thing." Bridget held the phone for a moment and then she decided to cheer him up. "Hey check your email for me will you," She said smiling to herself. She had sent him some photos of her laying on their bed biting her bottom lip while her hand was laying on her hip. She was dressed in sexy lingerie. When he seen the photos his whole demeanor changed and he became extremely excited. "Oh my god babe, you are so sexy," He told her over the phone. "Do you want to see more?" She asked him. "Hell yes I do, you have more?" He asked excitedly. "Yes, but it will cost you," She giggled. "Oh yeah, like what?" He asked curiously. "Just a few days with me and your daughter soon. Being away from you is killing me in more ways than one," She said in a sexy voice. "Baby, I know I am sorry. I wish you could be here with me right now. If we waited to have kids you could be," James said sadly. "It is ok, we both know we wouldn't change Megan for the world," She said longing to kiss her husband. "That is so true, now about these other pictures. Tell me you are in a state of undress?" He asked with a giggle. Bridget laughed as she emailed him the rest of the photos and she breathed the words, "Yes and I hope you enjoy them." When he received the photos he told her exactly what he was going to be doing with those photos. But, he asked her to talk to him while he did it. She began talking sexy to him and she couldn't help but to get turned on herself. She slid her hand down the front of her panties as she talked to James. He also had his hand inside his jeans rubbing himself. They both talked until each other was completely satisfied. "You realize when I get home I am going to have to make love to you all day?" He told her after they were finished. "Promises, promises," She said with a small laugh. As each said good night they both felt their hearts ache as they wished they could be in each other's arms. James really missed Megan, she was still a baby and he didn't want to miss out on any good times with her. Laying down on his bed at the hotel he got tears in his eyes when he realized his hobby and his family he always wanted wasn't on the same level like he dreamed it would be. He knew the other guys felt the same. However, Giselle was able to meet up with the band in different cities to spend time with Cullen since they didn't have kids. During one of the concerts James was playing his guitar and singing when all the sudden he thought of the photos Bridget had sent him. He felt himself getting excited and he couldn't stop it. Before he knew it there it was in front of this huge crowd, a boner that stretched all the way down his left thigh. He hoped nobody would notice, but being as big as he was there was no way to easily hide it. He noticed a lot of the women in the front smiling and whispering to each other. Then the photos on their cell phones started. He knew what they were snapping photos of. Sure enough a few days later when Bridget did research online to see how everyone was liking the Hangman's Noose's tour………. there it was, photos of James' boner going down his leg. A lot of things were being said on the net about it, all good for the guy. But, Bridget felt sick to her stomach. She looked at Cindy and Olivia and said, "Here we go. All these damn sluts have even more ammo to go after him now! How shitty this is, how incredibly shitty!" Bridget screamed upset. "Bridget, please calm down," Olivia said rubbing her back. "Why tell her to calm down? She has a right to be upset. Look at the shit these girls are saying about her husband," Cindy said looking at the computer screen. "Cindy, that doesn't mean James has done anything wrong." Olivia said trying to give Cindy a look to stop it. "Oh really, Olivia, if that was Marcus out there with his boner hanging down his leg and these girls were saying this stuff, you wouldn't be upset?" Olivia stared at Bridget for a minute after she asked her that question and she said, "I would be lying if I said it wouldn't bother me." Bridget put her hand on her forehead trying to think of what this is going to turn out to look like. While the whole time a camera man had his camera right in their faces. "Will you please get that damn thing out of my face?" Bridget asked the camera guy as she looked away. Suddenly, her phone rang, it was James. "Hello," She said with her upset tone. "Hey baby, how are you?" James asked as Bridget held the phone for a moment and then turned her back to the camera man as she spoke low into the phone. "I am not good. Did you know you are all over the internet? And it isn't about your music, it's about your big dick!" The girls couldn't help but laugh in the background. "I am sorry Bridget, I figured this would happen I seen several ladies smiling and taking photos," He said trying to explain. "What, so you enjoyed it? Why the hell would you be getting a damn hard on anyway?" She asked angrily as James began to get frustrated. "Bridget, would you calm down? First off no I am not enjoying this you know I don't flaunt my shit that way. And second, I was thinking of those damn photos you sent me last night," He said while Bridget rolled her eyes. "Oh, sure like I am supposed to believe that!" Bridget said very loudly. "Will you please stop being so mad at me I didn't do anything wrong, I can't control my boner no man can, you know this!" He said angrily. "Well at least someone is getting close enough to lust after you since I haven't seen you now for 3 weeks!" She snapped back hanging up on James. She rushed out of the room to get away from the cameras as her phone began ringing again. When it stopped ringing Cindy's phone began to ring. "Cindy, its James can you put her on the phone please?" He begged as Cindy looked around the room. "I think you are going to have to call back in a while she is really upset and I think she is changing Megan. Now can you put Matt on for a minute," Cindy kindly asked him. "Sure," James said shaking his head and handing the phone to Matt. "Hello my darling wife!" Matt said in a chipper mood. "Wow, it is nice to see how you guys lighten up when you are away from your wives," Cindy nastily said. "What, really Cindy? Don't tell me you are pissed, what the hell did I do?" Matt asked her surprised by her attitude. "Nothing, Mathew, absolutely nothing. It is good to hear your voice and all but I guess I will get off here for now." After they said their goodbye's Cindy felt like this wasn't the marriage she signed up for.

CHAPTER 13

The guys didn't understand why their wives were so upset. They knew the distance thing was going to be hard, but they had no idea what was really eating at the girls. It was pure jealousy mixed with aggravation. Why didn't their husband's seem to miss them as much? All the girls had to do was sit around taking care of their kids in front of the camera. Nothing fun or special about it. Then, they realized things were about to get even worse. The Hillenbrand guys found out about James, Marcus and Cullen being out of town. They planned to take full advantage of that fact. It was now nearly the end of September and the guy's tour was extended to December. The girls were heart broken, only talking by email and phone was getting old. They wanted to feel their husband's arms around them. By this point the guys were starting to feel the pain as well. Going a few months without their wives made it very hard on certain parts of their anatomy. The guys were all totally faithful to their ladies. The only one getting any sex from time to time was Cullen since Giselle could travel. Megan was almost seven months old and she was now crawling. Bridget took her to a small clothing store to do some shopping. She had no idea she would run into Billy at this type of store. He was a few feet behind her when she put Megan down for a moment to grab a shirt off the rack. In that amount of time Megan had crawled over to where Billy was standing with a cowboy hat on. "Come here darling you don't want to go over there," He said to Megan as Bridget spun around to look behind her. She began to feel a little foolish for putting her down. "Oh gosh, give me my daughter please," She said as she reached out to take Megan out of Billy's arms. "She is a little angel," He said as she snatched her out of his hands. "You know, you don't have to be such a bitch to me. I am trying to be friendly," He said looking at her with his hat popped upright from Megan grabbing it. "Friends? From what I hear you aren't friends with women. You use them for what they can give you." He stared at her for a moment and said, "That is not true and I take offense to that. All these women I am with know what they are getting into I don't take advantage." Bridget rolled her eyes as she dropped the shirt on the rack and began to walk out the door with Megan. "Hey, what are you going to do without your husband around? I mean I am sure it can get a little lonely," He said following her out the door. "Are you actually serious right now? You actually have the gall to come on to me while I hold my little girl. You really think I would cheat on my husband for a disgusting romp with you?" She asked showing her disgust. He thought for a second and said, "Why not? I mean you know he is fucking all the women he can get that big dick in." She turned around appalled after she fastened Megan in her seat. "You are a disgusting pig, you big jerk just go away and leave me alone," She said pushing him out of the way. "No really, I don't believe in infidelity. But, I am sure Mackenvoy won't be able to keep it in his pants while he is away. How about we wager on it?" Billy yelled to her as she ignore him getting into her car. Frazzled she grabbed her keys. While she was shaking she shoved them in the key hole. Speeding off she thought about what Billy was saying and the same thoughts popped in her head as before. Why would that asshole say those things to me? He must know I am not that pretty if my husband can be tempted by all those prettier women. When she pulled into her drive way she stared at the empty looking house and started to cry. The whole incident was caught on video because a camera man was following Billy that particular day. Bridget begged her family not to watch the show, she didn't want them seeing any of the stuff that happened on it. Billy felt confident as he walked back to his jeep. He loved messing with any of the Mackenvoy wives. He never intended on bedding them. He knew they would stay faithful to their husbands, but he did get enjoyment out of causing trouble. He used to mess around with Jackie in the same way when she was James' girl, but then he lost interest when he noticed the relationship wasn't up to par. Billy and Walker had no intentions for marriage or a serious relationship. And now that the show was hitting the air, their blog pages were filling up with women wanting a piece of them. All their address were kept private, but still there was the occasional nut that would show up in their town and find out where they filmed. Walker would sleep with many women, while Billy slept with some and only accepted fellatio from most. He thought it was safer in the long run from diseases or women trying to get pregnant by him. They would always use protection, but they knew that wasn't always fool proof. Joey was more of a lover. He wanted to find love and have kids. That following spring would be a real test for Joey. After Bridget put Megan to bed for a nap she sat at the kitchen table staring out the back door. She was so sad and she felt lost. She called up Olivia to tell her about the Billy incident and she tried to reassure her that Billy is always up to no good and not to worry. She completely understood though, because Walker worked on her the same way if he seen her out in public. That night as Bridget laid down to go to sleep she hoped she would soon see her husband. Around midnight the front door to Bridget's house swung open. Quietly, James tried to sneak in with his guitar case. Switching the alarm off not to wake her, he rushed up the stairs. He first went to see Megan. Looking at her sleeping in the light of the night light, tears formed in his eyes. He missed her so much he just wanted to pick her up and squeeze her but he knew he couldn't. Leaning down over her he gently kissed her on the forehead and smelled her blonde hair that was just like his. "Daddy loves you baby girl," He whispered before sneaking out of the room. He walked into the master bedroom tiptoeing. He stared at Bridget sleeping in the moonlight. Taking off his shirt and his pants he watched her chest move up and down as she lay on her back peacefully. He slid into bed and grabbed her up in his arms smelling the skin on her neck. She jerked awake and realized it was James. The smell of his cologne and skin made her heart skip a beat. She missed him so much. She couldn't wait to kiss him, they passionately kissed and hugged one another. "Oh god, James, I missed you so much," She cried as she spoke. "I know baby, I am so sorry. I missed you too. I couldn't wait to be in your arms like this," He whispered to her. Bridget wrapped her arms around his body. "Make love to me, please, make love to me I need to feel you to know you are real," She said as he started to take off her night shirt and panties. As he kissed and licked her all over she tried her best not to make too much noise. Her body was so sensitive from not being touched for so long by him. She grabbed his hair as he licked all over her body with his tongue, raising her thighs to lick every area he could. He rubbed her body with his fingertips running them between her thighs, watching her facial expressions as he was pleasuring her continuously. He was getting so excited he thought he would explode right then, just by watching the pleasure he was causing her. When he entered deep inside of her he could feel how hot and full of passion she was. He nearly almost climaxed himself just by becoming one with her in that second. He wanted to go fast and thrust hard in her, but he didn't want to hurt her and he didn't want this moment to end too soon. He missed her so much, he just wanted to be one with her all night long. Looking into her eyes he rocked slowly in and out of her, feeling her tighten around him every time she climaxed. Licking her neck as he tried to get his mind off of how good she felt, he couldn't hold it any longer. He began pumping harder grabbing her hair in his fist as he went deeper and faster. She was yelling out in pleasure as he started to climax she quickly breathed the words, "Please, don't do it inside me." He hurried up and pulled out of her just as he climaxed. "I'm sorry," She said breathless, "I am not using any birth control right now." James was breathing heavily as well as he said, "It's ok, I don't think we could handle another baby right now. I need to get to know Megan still." He smiled as he kissed her deeply. He wrapped his strong arms around her in a spoon position and they fell into a deep sleep. Olivia was about to be surprised as well. She had just gotten Justin back to sleep when she heard something by the front door. Grabbing her .38 special handgun from the night stand she started down the dark hallway to the front door area. "Who is there?" She said with a shaky voice. Nobody answered back. "Listen, you asshole I will blow you away if you don't get the hell out of here!" She shouted raising her voice. Opening the door slowly Marcus peeked around the side of the door and said, "Olivia it's me be quiet you are going to wake the twins." Olivia sat the gun down on the counter and shouted, "AHHHH, Marcus! Oh baby, I missed you so much!" She ran up to him and began kissing him profusely. "We need to try to be quiet sweetheart so we don't wake the babies. So much for surprising you," Marcus said as she kissed his face all over. "Oh god, Marcus, I thought you guys were going to be gone longer," She said in between kissing him. "Yeah we ended up not booking those venues. We wanted to get home. We will hit them next time. And we didn't tell you girls this because we wanted it to be a surprise, but we didn't know it would be so late when we got in," He explained to her. Olivia stared at him with sad eyes. "You need to make love to me now you big dope," She said grabbing his shirt and pulling him close. She grabbed his crotch while she kissed him and he immediately became excited. Massaging him in her hand she got down on her knees. He threw his head back and said, "Oh god yes, I missed you honey." While she pleasured him he grabbed her hair to keep it out of her face. After a minute he lifted her up and sat her on bar stool in their kitchen. "Come here," He whispered to her wiping the hair off her face. He started to kiss her hard as he pulled off her panties. "I have wanted you for so long, Olivia," He said rushing to get his pants down. When he pushed himself inside her, she tensed up grabbing a hold of his back. He started grinding hard up inside of her as she dug her nails into his back. They both made a lot of moaning noises as he thrust in and out of her. He reached under her butt cheeks to lift her up in the air as she wrapped her legs around him. He carried her to the bedroom laying her down on the bed. He began tasting her body all over gently with his tongue. She nibbled on her fingers as he bathed her with his tongue. She pulled him by his shirt he still had on and began kissing him deeply as he wrapped her legs around his hips. He rocked gently in and out of her. His thrusting became faster when he felt himself get ready to climax. Afterward he fell back on the bed out of breath. Breathing heavily he told her he loved her so much. She lay on his chest running her hands up and down it as they talked for a while before falling asleep. Cindy wasn't so happy to see Matt at first. He woke her up by licking up her thigh and pulling her panties off to the side. She popped her head up when she felt him. When she realized who it was she was so happy to see him, but also frustrated. "Oh, Matt. I am surprised to see you are back already," She said with a sleepy voice. Then she began to moan in pleasure as he kissed her body. He played around her with his tongue as he rubbed her breasts gently. "You still mad at me?" He said as he stopped and looked up at her with his sad puppy dog eyes. "Yes, I am very mad. But, right now I want some hot make up sex," She said as she pushed him onto his back. "Now, it is my turn to be in control," She said holding his arms down on the bed above his head. Biting his chest and neck she moved her way up to his face. "I should slap you, but all I want to do is make love to you. I have missed you so much," She paused so she could look into his eyes. "I have missed you too, Cindy, more than you can imagine," He said to her. She stared at his face for a moment and then let his arms go.

She reached down and grabbed him in her hand moving him into her. He gasped as she started to ride up and down in a fast manner. He grabbed a hold of her hips and pumped upright making her shout out. He felt her wetness run down all over him. Reaching up to grab a hold of her face with both hands he told her to open her eyes and look at him. "I would never forget you while I am away. This is what I have been dreaming about since I left," He said as he pumped harder. She continued to ride up and down on him feeling the thrusts become quicker. When she started to feel herself release again he let out a loud moan as he exploded with her. Laying down beside him she thought about how upset she was with him, but that could wait for now. She just wanted to hear his heartbeat as she lay on his chest holding each other all night.

CHAPTER 14

The next Halloween party was coming up soon along with the other holidays. The band promised to not make any more tour dates until the following year. This time was for family plain and simple. The television cameras were still following everyone around which made things extremely uncomfortable. But, the more people would tune in the better the price tag for charitable donations. Even though the band was staying home for now, they were working on their next album. Practice would be held at James' house in his basement every day after work. In March the producers of the show thought it would be a good idea to beef things up. So they asked the public for ideas on what they would like to see both families do on air. With the few fights that were aired on television the public didn't know the actual competition fights both families would hold every other summer throughout the years. These fights would have a man from each side of the family fight until one wasn't standing. The fights were brutal. Punching and throwing was allowed. Just no hits in the groin area, which none of the men did anyway. The following year these fights were to be viewed on television. They all would win their fair share of fights, but Cullen and Billy almost never lost a fight. They had never yet been teamed up to fight each other. Cullen had his turn with Joey and Walker, but never Billy yet. The next two years were calm somewhat. There were always the little spats between the Hillenbrands and Mackenvoys. Jackie was still trying to invade on James and Bridget's marriage, but they felt so deeply connected nobody was going to break that bond. The band had a few more tours to do as they were up to their third album release. They were becoming very famous along with the show. Everyone in the U.S knew who these two families were. Mostly they were known for their grace and kindness where charity was concerned. This was extremely important to both families. They didn't want the public to just see them for their fighting and not getting along with each other. In 2004 Megan and Shaina were turning 2 years old and the twins were 3. Cullen and Giselle never married, but she became pregnant with their first and only child, a son they would later name Caleb. Monica Hillenbrand had her second child as well, a girl named Rae. That March there was a terrible secret that Emma was keeping. None of the family could know about it. One day Walker couldn't hold his enthusiasm any longer. He seen Cullen and Marcus at the café getting their daily coffee before work. Walking in with a huge smile on his face he stood at the counter staring them down. "What the hell do you want, Opie?" Marcus asked adding creamer to his coffee. Cullen turned around to face Walker and gave him a quick smirk and then turned his back to him. "Look at you. Standing there all like your shit don't stink," Walker said leaning on the counter, "If it wasn't for you I would still have my beautiful cousin, Rachel. Uncle Walter don't even live in this town anymore cause it is too painful, you son of a bitch." Marcus dropped his stir stick. "Walker, why don't you let the shit go? He isn't the one responsible for Rachel's death and you know exactly what I am talking about," Marcus said hatefully. "Oh, is that right you piece of shit?" Walker asked. Cullen turned toward Walker again staring him down. Walker took his elbow off the counter and moved toward Cullen shoulder checking him. "Eye for eye, asshole," Walker whispered into Cullen's ear as he walked off disappearing into the patron area of the café. Marcus and Cullen looked at each other. "I wonder what the hell that was supposed to mean," Marcus said staring at Cullen. They were both smart men and knew that the Hillenbrand's never started anything without good reason. Grabbing their coffees they headed to the office where James was already busy at work. Colton and Rick were in Colton's office having a small meeting. Marcus hurried to James' office to tell him about the encounter with Walker. "What the hell do you think that means?" James asked Marcus. "It sounds cryptic as hell to me and I think we need to go talk to daddy about it. Cullen is already in there waiting for us," Marcus said as James hopped up from his desk chair. Walking at a fast pace to Colton's office, Cullen was already warning them about what Walker had said. "Well that sounds to me like he is going after my little girl or possibly one of your wives," Colton grumbled with a cigar hanging out of this mouth. "What do you want me to do?" Rick asked. "Nothing, I think I will leave this up to my boys," Colton said looking at Marcus and James. "Us, why? I have my law practice and kids to raise, daddy, I don't have time to be a babysitter to Emma," Marcus said in a hateful manner. Colton's eyes veered over to James. "What, me?" James said pointing at his chest. "If you love your baby sister you will do this. Eye for an eye would mean something deeply personal so I don't think he is after your wives. I think he is after Emma," Rick said. Cullen stood staring at the floor feeling like it was all his fault. "Fucking Walker, why don't I just go kick his ass and put him in the hospital? That will keep him away from her," Cullen grumbled. Colton became frustrated and said, "Cullen that will just cause more trouble. I think we need to just follow Emma and see what happens." Colton spun around in his chair to look out the window. "But, if that dirty son of bitch touches my daughter there will be hell to pay," Colton added with a dead expression on his face. What nobody knew was the affair was in full force already. Emma was in love and she couldn't stop how she felt. Packard and Jack knew nothing about the love affair either. Only a select few knew about it in the Hillenbrand clan. For the next week Colton gave James time off of work so he could follow Emma. He never told Bridget he was doing this. He knew she would be against it and he didn't want her to worry about the fighting that was sure to ensue. By the third day he hit pay dirt. He followed Emma to a rundown barn out in the country on the Hillenbrands side of town. When he parked in a place she couldn't see him he snuck up to the barn window to look inside. He could not believe what he was seeing. Shaking his head in disbelief, he angrily stomped to the barn door and walked inside shouting, "What the hell is going on here?" Emma jumped turning around startled. "James! Oh god, James please don't tell daddy he will kill me," She begged terrified. James just stared at her, "Do you think? What the hell is wrong with you sis? How could you do this to us? And you, I am shocked at what you are doing here lover boy," James looked passed Emma to stare down none other than Joey Hillenbrand. "Look, I love your sister," Joey started to say. "Oh, don't make me fucking puke. This isn't love and you know it isn't!" James shouted. "The hell it isn't. I don't just hop into bed with anyone…" Joey didn't have a chance to complete his sentence when Emma spoke up, "He is right, James, this isn't something dirty." James became angrier, "Emma, get your little ass in the car. You are too young to know what love is," James ordered her. "I am 20 years old I think I know how I feel!" Emma shouted back. "Emma, go ahead and get in the car and go," Joey pushed her as James rolled his eyes. Emma walked up to James and grabbed his arm, "Come on lets go. I don't want you fighting…. please big brother." She tugged on his arm as he continued to stare at Joey. "I will be seeing you," James said as he turned to leave the barn with Emma. As soon as James got in his car to follow Emma back to town he called up Colton to tell him the bad news. Colton was livid. He was extremely disgusted with the fact that Joey had been with his daughter. And worse yet, making her fall in love with him. Emma was so upset. She loved Joey and her father ordered her not to see him anymore. But, Joey did in fact feel the same way about her. It wasn't revenge or a piece of tail to him, it was love. Walker and Billy knew all about the affair. And once Colton knew about it, Packard would know as well. Joey told Walker the Mackenvoys knew all about the affair so he told Packard. Packard called Joey and asked him to come to his house. The Hillenbrand manor was smaller than the Mackenvoys and more modest, but still big. It sat on 80 acres, down a wooded lane where nobody could see the house from the road. A sign sat at the beginning of the driveway simply stating "Trespassers will be shot". As Joey drove down the long lane he knew he was going to be in trouble. When he went inside Packard sat at the kitchen table with a mean look on his face. "Well, I am sure you know," Joey said staring at him. Slowly Packard stood from his seat and walked over in front of Joey. Looking at him for a few seconds he punched him square in the nose. "Boy, what the hell is wrong with you? Are you that desperate or just that stupid?" He yelled as he knocked Joey to the floor. Lisa came running into the room. She didn't say a word, she just stared at both of the men. "I am sorry, daddy. I just….. I feel like I love her truly," Joey said lying on the floor. "Don't give me that shit!" Packard said waving his hand up into the air. "We don't have anything to do with that family and you know this. I am not about to become in-laws with that worthless son of a bitch, Colton!" Lisa felt like she should intervene so she calmly said, "Packard, please be easy." Walking over to help Joey up off the floor she looked at Packard, "He will end it, won't you?" She looked at Joey as he stared at the kitchen table. "Yeah, momma, I will end it," He said hatefully. When Emma arrived at Colton and Victoria's house with James she felt very uneasy. Neither of them said a word. Emma walked into the house first to see her mother standing stone cold in the living room staring at her. "My darling little girl. How could you be so stupid? I didn't raise you to run around with farm animals. I raised you to be a good girl," Victoria said as tears welled up in her eyes. "I am sorry, momma," Emma said staring down at the floor in shame. "You better be more than sorry, little girl," Colton said as he walked into the room. "From now on you are to let me or your momma know at all times where you are. Obviously, we can't trust you not to run around with that worthless scum bucket. You get your ass out of my sight I don't want to look at you right now," Colton said shooing her away. Crying, Emma ran out of the living room to her bedroom. As James got ready to open the door to leave Colton spoke up, "Son, I want you to follow her for the next two weeks." James let out a long sigh, "Come on, daddy, I don't have time for this shit I have the band." Colton rudely interrupted raising his voice, "Family is more important than some silly band. Now you do what I tell you and I don't want to hear another word about it." When James made it home that night he told Bridget what had happened. She was extremely upset that he kept it from her for the past week. He apologized, but she felt so left out like she wasn't a part of the family. "Honey, Olivia didn't even know about this. We wanted to be sure Emma was messing around with someone before we mentioned it. And the first time I seen her with him was today," He tried to explain. Bridget sat angry for a minute, "I don't want you keeping stuff from me James. No matter how silly it may seem, please don't keep things from me." James dropped his head in shame and said, "I promise I won't keep anything from you anymore." A few days later, Marcus and James showed up where Joey was by himself at the feed store buying oats for their horses. James grabbed Joey's arm and twisted it behind his back and wrapped his arm around his throat while Marcus jumped in his face grabbing him by the face. "You keep your dick out of my sister you son of a bitch, because if you don't you are going to be taught a horrible lesson and I can't promise we will be fair about it," Marcus threatened. Joey grunted as James choked him and put pressure on his arm. "What would a judge say about this? A fancy lawyer such as yourself," Joey stuttered out in a joking voice. "Don't get smart it doesn't become you. Stay away from my baby sister you fucking scum," Marcus grumbled as he started to walk away. James let go of his arm punching him in the back of the head. "You fucking asshole, you almost broke my arm," Joey said while he was getting back up off the ground. James looked over his shoulder and whispered, "Pussy." Olivia was just as upset with the situation. Being in this family was difficult on both girls. They would often discuss how yucky the feeling was that they never knew what was going to happen next. For the next month James followed Emma. It was very tiring for him since he had a job plus he was to be going on tour again the next two months. During the next family picnic at the Mackenvoy manor, Emma seemed different. Bridget wasn't paying too much attention to Emma since Victoria invited Jackie to the barbecue. All she kept doing was watching how Jackie stared at James. It made her sick. Emma walked over and told James she needed to speak to him and Marcus up at the barn. When she started to walk up to the barn James looked over at Bridget and motioned with his head for her to come too. Bridget looked at Olivia and said, "Let's go." When they were all in the barn, Marcus started to giggle when he talked about the stuff he and James did to get spankings in that barn. Marcus was standing in front of her while James was beside her. The girls stayed by the entry way. "I am scared," Emma started to say. "Oh no this can't be good," James said looking at Bridget. "Well, let's hear it Em, we aren't getting any younger," Marcus pushed. "I'm pregnant," She whispered under her breath. Olivia and Bridget looked at each other shocked. "What did you just say?" Marcus shouted. "Oh my god you are still fucking him!" James yelled. "NO! Honest, I haven't seen him," Emma said scared. "James, please take it easy," Bridget whispered. "Alright everyone calm down and be quiet or someone is going to hear," Olivia warned. Marcus thought for a moment then looked up, "You are going to have an abortion. That is all there is to it." Both girls gasped. "Marcus, no I can't believe you would say that!" Olivia said in disgust. Bridget just stood with her mouth wide open. "She has no choice, Liv, she can't have a Hillenbrand baby daddy will kill her!" Marcus shouted. James shook his head, "There won't be an abortion come on." James grabbed Emma by the arm and walked her out of the barn. "What.... what are you doing, James?" Emma asked in a scared voice. "You are going to tell daddy right now," He said still holding her by the arm as they walked down the hillside. "No, please big brother, he will kill me," Emma whimpered. "You should have thought about that before," James grumbled. Bridget followed behind calling James' name softly. Marcus and Olivia followed behind as they all walked up to the picnic tables.

CHAPTER 15

Emma jerked away from James as they stood directly in front of Colton. "What the hell are you two fighting about?" Colton grumbled as he took a drink of his beer. Marcus strolled up mentioning, "This isn't going to be good." James stared at Emma and then back to his father. "Emma has something she has to tell you," James said to Colton. She stared at her daddy with dread filling up her stomach. Her chest felt heavy with anxiety as she started to open her mouth, "I'm so sorry, daddy, I haven't been seeing Joey anymore I swear! But, I am pregnant and I am so sorry daddy," Emma cried in her hands. James and Marcus looked at their father wondering what was going to come next. Victoria stood up rigid and began shaking. "Get yourself into the house young lady," Victoria said as tears welled up in her eyes. Emma ran to the house as Victoria followed her. Colton began to stand up slowing raising the sleeves up on shirt and started to walk toward Marcus and James, "I asked you two to do one fucking thing and you couldn't keep your damn sister out of trouble?" He said stomping towards his boys. "Grab the kids let's get inside!" Olivia yelled to Bridget. They ran inside with the kids, but Bridget turned around just in time to see Colton punch James in the face. Marcus and James both were yelling they were sorry, but they took each hit from their father without resistance. Olivia covered Amanda's eyes as she cradled her pushing Justin in the door. Jackie stepped back from the table and watched in horror. When Olivia and Bridget got into the house Victoria was yelling at Emma and she smacked her hard across the face. "You are going to get rid of that monstrosity growing in your belly so help me god!" Victoria shouted with daggers in her eyes. Emma didn't say a word. Olivia kept peeking out the window. "Please…. stop hitting them," Olivia said in a whimpering voice. Bridget sat in disbelief staring at the living room floor. Olivia quickly ran to sit down on the sofa next to Bridget and said, "Oh god oh god oh god this is bad, Bridget, this is so bad." Olivia squeezed her hands together rocking back and forth while Bridget sat transfixed on the carpet. Emma ran to her bedroom in shame as Victoria came stomping into the living room and shouted, "Yes, this is bad. If my sons weren't so busy with that ridiculous band my daughter wouldn't be pregnant. If you were decent wives they would just plan on being successful men, not little boys following a silly dream." Both girls stared up at Victoria while the kids played around the room not knowing what was going on around them. As Victoria left the room, the front door opened. Marcus came walking in with a busted nose and swollen eye. "Oh, god Marcus baby I am so sorry," Olivia said running up to him to kiss his face. He shook his head and said, "Let's just go, I want to get out of here right now." Bridget looked up at Marcus with worry on her face. "Where is James?" She asked him with a shaky voice. "He went walking off to the pond," Marcus said as he picked up Justin. Bridget began to stand up. "Can you watch Megan for one minute while I go talk to him? I won't be too long," She asked looking at Olivia. "I wouldn't bother, he is embarrassed. I think he wanted to be alone, but Jackie followed him," Marcus said in a flat tone. Bridget just stared at Marcus with her heart dropping to her stomach. She felt like she should be the one comforting her husband. Marcus looked at her for a minute and then he and Olivia started out the door. "Usual life in the Mackenvoy house," Marcus said as he shut the door. Bridget lifted up Megan in her arms and began to cry. All the sudden the side door in the dining room opened, it was Colton. Bridget glanced at him with tears in her eyes still holding onto Megan. He looked at her as he calmly sat down at the kitchen table. "My kids….. they are my pride and joy. I know you don't agree with how I do things, but those boys needed to be taught a lesson. I mean, if they did what I asked and if they weren't so involved with that ridiculous band," He just stopped and shook his head. Bridget sat rubbing Megan's back listening to Colton. He looked over at her, "Well don't you have something to say?" He asked her. "No. It doesn't matter what I think or say," She whispered standing up to carry Megan out the door. She walked outside and looked around not seeing James anywhere. She went over to the car and fastened Megan into the car seat. Waiting for twenty minutes she figured he wasn't coming back anytime soon and Jackie would be more than thrilled to give him a ride. She started the car sadly staring off into the direction James disappeared to. Waiting a few more minutes until nobody came, she finally backed up and drove home crying. After putting Megan to bed for a nap she sat down at her kitchen table. Not believing what she had just seen. Not to mention the fact her husband left her sitting there with his ridiculous family, but allowing Jackie to comfort him. She had so many emotions. She felt sick and angry. Grabbing her phone she called the one person who was always there for her, Jon. Waiting on the answer nervously, she bit her lip. "Hello," She heard a sleepy voice on the other end. "Jon?" She said. "Yeah, hey Bridget how are you doing?" He said with cheer filling his voice. "It is so good to hear your voice," He said as she just sit crying, trying not to let him hear. "Bridget, are you there?" She paused and finally said, "Yes, I am here." She looked up at the ceiling with tears rolling down her cheeks. She explained to Jon what had happened and how she didn't know how James was. Jon tried to be as comforting as he could be. "Do you want me to come see you?" He asked her. "Yes, please come see me. I need a friend that isn't a part of this family," Bridget begged. "Ok, listen let me talk to my girl and I will see if she is ok with me coming down there here in two days. I promise I will try to be there for you as soon as I can," He said with concern in his voice. "Thank you, Jon," She said quietly. After saying their goodbyes as she hung up her cell phone the front door creaked open. James came walking in slowly. He had a hat on and was looking down at the floor as he walked up to the kitchen table. She calmly sat her cell phone down. "Are you ok?" She asked. He raised his head up where she could barely see his eyes under the bill of his hat. "I am sorry I didn't want you to drive home without me," He said sheepishly. "Megan was tired and I didn't want to sit there with your parents," She said angrily. She could see that James eye was going to be black for sure and he had a busted lip. He pulled out a chair and slid it over so he could look her in the eyes. He grabbed the hat off his head and laid it on the table. "I was embarrassed. I didn't want you to see me that way," He said in a low voice. Bridget got upset and gave out a sigh, "I am your wife. I am supposed to be there for you, good or bad. Or did you forget that?" She asked as he shook his head. "No, I didn't forget that. I didn't want to see the look in your eye knowing how my family does things," He mumbled. She kept her arms folded as he made a half ass attempt to explain. "So, you hide from me. Like you always do. You hide everything from me," She tearful grumbled. He started to feel like he was losing what was most precious to him. "No, it wasn't like that, please don't think that," He said sadly. "What happened with Jackie? Was she comforting enough? Did she make everything ok?" Bridget's voice started to crack. He closed his eyes and started to rub his face. "I didn't want her to follow me in fact, I asked her to go away. She followed me the whole time. It isn't what you think," He said trying to make her feel not so threatened by the whole situation. Bridget sighed loudly and said, "I will never really know will I?" She stood up and started to walk away from the table when James grabbed her arm and said, "Wait baby, please don't leave things like this." She pulled her arm away from him frustrated and said, "James, I am tired I am going to take a bath. I need to wash this shit feeling off of myself." James stayed sitting at the table staring at the floor with tears in his eyes. He stood up and walked up the back stairs to their bedroom, he couldn't leave things this way. He went into the master bathroom where Bridget was already sitting in her bubble bath soaking and feeling terrible. "Bridget, I love you and I am sorry. I have never been humiliated in front of you by my father before and I am sorry that I don't know the exact way to handle that kind of situation. I didn't want Jackie bothering me, believe me she just wouldn't go away. I know daddy loves us, he just gets mixed up at how to be a good daddy when it comes to that other family," James tried to explain as Bridget sat listening. Then she looked up at him and said, "So is this the kind of father you will be to Megan? Will you be this brutal and controlling with her?" She asked afraid of what his answer was going to be. Kneeling down next to her he shook his head and said, "I would never hurt my daughter or a son the way daddy hurt me. And I would like to think my kids would be smart enough to stay away from Hillenbrand people." Bridget rolled her eyes. "I don't want to talk about this anymore," She said leaning her head back and closing her eyes. "We have to talk about this. I don't want to ignore anything in this marriage I want it to work. I want us to have at least four to six kids and be a happy family," James said while Bridget quickly looked at him, "Four to six kids?" He smiled and shook his head yes. "I love you and I want you to have as many of my babies as you can," He said biting his bottom lip. She stared at him with her mouth open. "Raise up," He said moving her forward so he could wash her back. "I promise you I will not leave you out of anything that happens from now on, I mean this Bridget. I will do whatever you want me to. I want you to feel safe and secure in our marriage, Okay?" He asked looking at her. "This is the last time James. No more I can't take any more of the secrecy or Jackie trying to take my place," She said as he washed her back. "Jackie will never take your place she isn't even in the running," He said as he leaned in to kiss her. When she pressed her lip against his top lip he pulled back grabbed his lip saying, "Ouch!" Bridget couldn't help but giggle. It didn't take long for Rick and Cullen to hear about Emma's pregnancy. Mare was much more accepting of the fact. After all it was an innocent baby. Everyone wondered what this would mean for Emma and the baby. Victoria couldn't have her daughter giving birth to a Hillenbrand baby. Emma made up her mind that she would not have an abortion. It was completely against what she believed in. Joey stayed away from Emma as he was told to do. Cullen felt extremely sad inside remembering Rachel and his unborn baby she took to her grave with her. He felt compelled to go see Emma. Emma was studying for her yearend exams when she heard a knock at the door. She opened the door to see Cullen. "Hey, how are you come on in?" She said inviting him in. Cullen walked in with his head down. "I really need to ask, how are you doing? Is Victoria here?" He asked looking around. Emma shook her head no. "I am doing ok I guess. I feel a little sick to my stomach, but I am doing okay physically wise," She said while Cullen smiled. "That is so good to hear little cousin. Listen I have to say I am here for selfish reasons," He said to her while she looked up at him. "Go on," She said. "I came mostly to beg you not to abort this baby, please. And don't let things get so bad that you feel there is no way out. I am always here and you always have my house to come to if you need to get away from Victoria or Uncle Colton," Cullen said to her with a kind look on his face. Emma smiled and gave him a big hug. "You are such a big softie, I love you so much," She said as he laughed. "I love you too and I mean what I am saying to you," He said as he stopped hugging her for a moment. She looked up at him with her pretty eyes. "I know you do. And I may take you up on it eventually once I start showing. I can't imagine momma wanting me here when she can see my sin right in her face," She said glancing down at her belly. He paused looking at her with a serious face and said, "A baby isn't a sin, it is a gift from god. Don't let her or anyone make you feel differently. My little boy is the light of my life and I can't help to think who my other child could have been." Emma rubbed Cullen's arm and said, "You don't need to feel guilty for what Rachel did." He began shaking his head, "Yes I do. If I hadn't abandoned her she would still be alive. But, that is something I will live with for the rest of my life. If anyone understands what you are going through being in love with the wrong type of person, it is me. Although I hate Joey, I know you feel love for him. I just hope you are able to get rid of it and not let it consume you. Just take good care of that angel growing inside you ok?" He said opening the door to leave. Emma smiled. "I will cousin and thanks for the advice and being here for me," She said before closing the door. Bridget got her chance to see her good friend Jon. James was at work when she got the call Jon was in town. Excitedly, Bridget got her stuff together and grabbed Megan to go see Jon at the café. He looked so good. Very muscular and clean cut. Of course, he had to be for the television roles he was getting. He enjoyed his job so much. Bridget felt good about that. Especially since she felt her not being in his personal life surely made things easier on him. They talked a lot about Bridget and James' relationship. Jon tried to be supportive, but he couldn't help reminding her maybe it was a mistake that she got involved with James. Jon had another reason for being in town besides to see Bridget. Their good friend from Indiana, Beverly, was getting married to a French guy she met on a trip. The wedding was going to be held in Kentucky only a couple hour drive for James and Bridget. Marcus, Olivia, Matt, Cindy, Cullen and Giselle were all invited as well. The day of Beverly's wedding was already full of tension. Bridget couldn't put her finger on it, but James was acting a little cool with her. At the reception Beverly asked Hangman's Noose to play some songs live. They obliged while Jon and Bridget danced to the music. James couldn't help to notice how happy Bridget seemed bouncing around with Jon. He caught Jon grinding his crotch area all up against Bridget's ass. He began to feel rage as he played his guitar. He was having trouble singing out the lyrics as he watched his wife and her former lover grind on the dance floor. After the set, James didn't see where Jon or Bridget disappeared to. The DJ began to play the song "Macarena" By Los Del Rio, when James noticed them across the room near the front exit to the building. Eyeing them over the heads of people dancing he watched Jon cup her face in his hands as he kissed her forehead. Livid, James ran through the crowd of people. He rushed up beside Jon and punched him in the side of the head. Jon fell to the floor as Bridget screamed for James to stop. Cullen and Marcus heard the commotion and ran to try to stop the fight. But, Jon and James were heavily into the fight. Throwing each other around the hallway causing damage to the building walls, they beat each other with force in the face and stomach. Cullen pushed Jon off of James and held him against the wall by the front door while Marcus pinned James up against the wall. Bridget looked at James angrily. She turned to Beverly and said, "I am so sorry about this we will pay for all the damages." Then she turned to James and shouted, "You promised me you wouldn't do this!" She stormed out the front door passing Jon without saying a word. As James ran out after Bridget Jon yelled out, "Looks like someone is in the doghouse tonight." Cullen pushed Jon harder against the wall and said, "Mind your own business dipshit." Cullen stayed in Jon's face for a moment before storming off. On the way home James nor Bridget spoke to one another for a while. As Bridget drove the long trip James couldn't hold his tongue anymore. "Why didn't you tell me Jon came to see you two days ago?" James asked as Bridget looked over confused. "What? Is that what this is all about? I didn't tell you because there is nothing to tell. He is a friend and he was coming down for the wedding anyway," She tried to explain. "Did you talk about what happened with me and daddy?" James asked. She was quiet for a moment. "Of course you did," He said angrily. "James I need people to talk to too. And after all you have Jackie," She said sarcastically. "No, no don't do that. You know how much she drives me crazy," He said grinding his teeth. "How the hell did you know I talked to Jon were you spying on me?" She asked while he paused for a moment. "No, momma told me. And why the hell did he have his junk all over you? And why the hell did he put his lips on your head?" James angrily shouted. Bridget huffed rolling her eyes, "First he was kissing me goodbye which I have seen Jackie do to you constantly and why is your freaky mother spying on me? Oh my god this is so fucked up!" She grumbled as she pulled the car into the driveway. She jumped out of the car with the house keys in her hand. "Come in here so I can clean you up," She ordered James. He sat down angrily at the kitchen table while she grabbed the first aid kit. "I don't want Megan to see her daddy with black eyes all the time. Thank god she is with Emma," She told him as she cleaned the gash above his eye. James seemed to ignore what she was saying as he began running his hand up her thigh. "You look so beautiful in this dress," He said as he reached her panties. "James, please I have to clean you up," She said pushing his hands away. He pulled her panties down to her ankles and pushed his head up under her short thigh high dress. Licking her she couldn't help but to feel excited as she gasped and breathed the words, "I am so mad at you I don't want to do this!" She paused for a moment enjoying the feel of his tongue on her and then she said, "Oh okay maybe I do want to do this." She reached down grabbing his face and kissing him passionately. Pulling at his tuxedo pants she unbuttoned them and began stroking him. She grabbed his hand and pulled him to the couch. She threw him down and took him in her mouth. Sucking up and down she would gag herself at times from the length of him. She sat down on top of him gasping as he entered her. She began riding fast and harder as she felt herself start to climax. "You are going to have to slow down I can't take it," He said breathlessly while she continued to grind hard on top of him. "I am not stopping it feels too good," She said as she started to orgasm again. He grabbed her hips and started pounding her hard up into the air. As she tried to hop off he kept her on top of him and said, "Don't you go anywhere you take it!" He pumped her harder upward as she moaned out in pleasure squeezing the back of the couch in her hand. He couldn't hold his orgasm back anymore as he exploded deep inside of her. Bridget fell forward onto his sweaty chest as they both breathed loudly. He wrapped his arms around her back and said, "I am sorry I am a jackass sometimes. I just love you so much, baby." She kissed his neck and said, "I love you too." They held one another on the couch as they both fell off to sleep.

CHAPTER 16

It was the end of May and it was time for the usual Memorial Day picnics both families would hold. Joey would try not to look over at Emma knowing she was carrying his baby in her belly. In fact, he was already seeing someone knew named Missy. She was pretty with shoulder length black hair and bright blue eyes. Emma tried her best not to feel hurt, but she understood. They both had to move on and that is what he was doing. The fight with Colton was to be buried in the past as far as Bridget was concerned. She didn't want to remember that. While everyone ate their food, Victoria pushed Emma to eat and drink. Emma let out a loud breath saying, "I just don't feel good, momma. I feel a little sick today." Victoria became frustrated and said, "If you aren't going to eat at least drink some lemonade I made for you." Emma took a few large gulps of her lemonade as Victoria watched. After finishing her lemonade Emma walked over to play with the kids in the park. While Emma spun Megan around in the air she felt a sharp pain in her lower belly. Grabbing a hold of her stomach she walked over to the picnic table. Doubling over in pain Olivia grabbed her arms holding her up. "Are you ok?" Olivia asked her watching how much pain she seemed to be in. All the sudden blood began to run down Emma's right thigh. "Oh my god, momma!" Emma screamed. Victoria walked over like nothing important was going on. "Come on my dear get in the car," She had the same robotic voice with no emotion at all. Bridget couldn't believe how emotionless and cold this woman was. Everyone else was very concerned for Emma's pain, but not Victoria. Even Colton seemed concerned for his daughter's apparent pain and picked her up into his arms as she sobbed. He carried her to the car and tried to help her in the passenger seat. Joey could hear her scream and looked over to watch the commotion. When he seen her hunched over getting into the car with blood running down her leg he knew. Billy came up behind him and slammed his hand down on his shoulder and said, "I am sorry brother. I don't think you will have to worry about that issue anymore." Looking at Billy, he then turned to walk off. Not being able to hold back the tears, he took a walk all on his own as Missy watched helplessly. Everyone was at the hospital waiting to hear the news on Emma. When they found out she had lost the baby, most were relieved in a sick way. But, Bridget stayed in Emma's hospital room for a minute to make sure she was okay. As Emma laid on her left side crying, Bridget knew she needed someone. She crawled in bed with her and wrapped her arms around her, "It will be okay. You are a strong woman and things happen for a reason. Maybe not always good things, but you will get through this I promise you." Emma just thanked her as she cried, being cradled by Bridget. Cullen stood in the doorway watching. He wanted to make it all go away for Emma, but he knew he couldn't. He could feel the same pain she was going through just by watching her. Cullen was grateful for Bridget's compassion since Emma's own mother couldn't muster it out for her. But, he wasn't aware that later on in their life, he and Bridget would need that same compassion for one another. Emma realized this did happen for a reason, no matter how painful it was. The news of the fight at Beverly's wedding hit the tabloid magazines and celebrity news stations fast. Seeing as though Jon and James were both popular in the celebrity world, it was relentless all the teasing that went on. Jon worried it would taint his reputation as a serious actor. The shows cameramen were still filming every week. Luckily, the fight with Colton and the miscarriage were not filmed. Unfortunately, the fight at the wedding was filmed by guests at the wedding. Once again, Victoria was not proud of this fact. She blamed Bridget as always. And it is true she did have her followed on occasion hoping to catch her doing something wrong to bring to James' attention. That summer James was to go on tour again with the band. Giselle wouldn't be able to travel this time now that Caleb was born. The tour took them to Germany one month into the tour. While the girls were alone Billy and Walker were relentless in their cat calls and harassing of them. Olivia and Bridget were walking towards the park when they heard Billy's jeep come pulling up beside them as they walked down the side walk. All the sudden he started blaring the song "Don't Turn Away" By Whitesnake. The girls began to walk faster, trying to get away. When Billy sped up his jeep, Walker asked with a laugh, "What the hell are you doing?" Billy glanced over at him smiling as he said, "Just watch." The girls started to run down the grassy hill off the side of the road to the park. The next thing they knew, the music started to get louder. When they turned around to look, Billy's jeep came flying down the hillside. The girls screamed as they ran off to the side, jumping out of the way. As he came to a stop Bridget shouted, "Are you crazy?" Billy didn't say a word as he looked at them singing the lyrics to the song. The girls ignored him and walked away disgusted. Billy laughed looking at Walker and said, "Don't you think Bridget has a nice ass? I wouldn't mind having a small taste." Billy continued to watch Bridget walk away. Walker laughed as they drove back up the hill. Disgusted, the girls walked through the park shocked at what had just happened. Jackie had landed herself a job as an assistant at the Mackenvoy business. Bridget was crushed when she found out James wouldn't be home for their anniversary. Neither would Matt for that matter. Cindy had already found out she was expecting again and Bridget knew she was as well. She knew exactly when it happened, the night of Beverly's wedding. The only way she was going to be able to tell James the good news was over the phone. It wasn't what she hoped for. She had tried calling him two days before their anniversary, but when they were able to talk he would rush her off the phone. Little did she know at the time, Victoria had sent Jackie over to Germany to take James and Cullen documents from work. She intended to stay and keep James company in between shows. When Bridget told Cindy how she was going to have to break the pregnancy news to James, Cindy told her she wouldn't bother telling Matt. "He will find out when the baby is born. I am so over this shit," Cindy grumbled. Bridget stood up fidgeting. "Today is my anniversary I am calling my husband to tell him the big news," Bridget said grabbing her phone. "Maybe this will get him to come home sooner," She said while dialing. The phone rang several times and finally an answer. "Hello," A female voice said on the other end. Bridget recognized this raspy voice. "Jackie? What the fuck are you doing with my husband's phone!?" Bridget yelled. "Calm down, I am here keeping them company and I had to bring them documents anyway. I figured I would stay the next night or two while they get things signed and stuff. Anyway, would you like to talk to James?" Jackie asked with a happy voice while Bridget held the phone feeling the vomit come up the back of her throat. As Jackie could be heard in the background shouting to James, Bridget threw down her cell phone and ran to the bathroom to throw up. Cindy grabbed the phone as Olivia came walking in the front door, "Hey girls what is up?" When she noticed Cindy had the phone to her ear she said, "Oh sorry I didn't know you were on the phone," Olivia sat down embarrassed of being so loud when she came in the door. She put the twins down on the floor to play with Megan and Shaina. "Hey baby, how are you?" James said on the other end. "Hmmm, this isn't baby," Cindy said sternly. "Oh, hey what's up?" James asked. "What's up? Nothing at all James, but we would like to know what is up with you? Why is psycho skank there?" Cindy asked with the same stern tone. "Momma sent her here with documents I had to sign that is all. Where is my wife?" James asked. "Your wife? Like you care, she is in the bathroom throwing up." Cindy said nonchalantly. "What?" James asked confused. "Yeah, that is right your wife you care so much about is making you a daddy again. Congratulations you jerk," Cindy said hanging up the phone before James had a chance to reply. Holding his phone in shock he started screaming happily at the top of his lungs. Cullen came running over to him, "Hey dude what is up we have to get ready to go on stage!" James still laughed and shouted, "Woo-Hoo! I am going to be a daddy again!" James excitedly began hugging Cullen. All the guys congratulated him while Jackie made a disgusted pinched face. As soon as the guys headed back on stage Jackie dialed Victoria to give her the news. James wanted to call Bridget back right away, but he had to play first. He was on fire when the band performed and everyone loved the show. The news was uplifting for him and he couldn't wait to get home and hug his wife. After Cindy hung up on James, Olivia just stared at her and said, "Wow you really do have a way with men don't you?" Cindy just laughed, "He deserves it. He is there with Jackie." Olivia's mouth gaped open. "What a bitch are you serious?" Olivia asked in shock. "Totally serious. He claims she just brought stuff for him to sign," Cindy replied. "Well…. it don't matter really Cindy, James isn't interested in Jackie. He never wanted her to have his babies. Only psycho momma Victoria does," Olivia said with a scratchy type scour. Just then Bridget walked into the living room pale faced. "Hi Olivia," She said sitting down gently. "Hey sweetie how are you feeling you don't look so good?" Olivia asked her. "I will be fine. I don't think it is morning sickness this time it is all about stress," Bridget said wiping her forehead. Cindy started to explain what James told her. "I heard, I don't care. I just don't care anymore," Bridget said interrupting Cindy, "My marriage is all about him, all about this crazy family. I have accepted that. It is no fairy tale." Everyone sat quiet for a moment. "Since both of you are pregnant I want to be too," Olivia said as Cindy laughed. "What are you laughing at? I think it would be neat us all pregnant at the same time again. The first time it happened with you two expecting together, I already had my twins. I want us all to be together. I am going to talk Marcus into it when he gets back. I am off the pill at the moment," Olivia said happily. Bridget just listened day dreaming at the floor. Once again those notorious video camera's filmed everything that was private to her. After the concert James continuously tried to call Bridget. He never got an answer. He knew she was hurt at him, he left several messages hoping she would call him back. He and the guys all shared a hotel room at a really nice hotel. It was a suite that attached to another room with four full size beds. Jackie was going to sleep on the sofa in the room. James laid back on his bed, exhausted and upset that he couldn't talk to Bridget. Jackie came walking over and slid into bed with him wrapping her arms around his waist. He stared up at the ceiling with tired watery eyes. Jackie talked to him for a bit about different things. As he listened he just stared at the ceiling. Closing his eyes he began to doze off to sleep. "I miss my wife, Jackie, I miss my little girl. I don't know how many more times I can do this," He whispered. She watched him fall asleep as he finished his sentence. She rubbed the side of his face and kissed him on the lips. "I love you," She told him. He let out a little snore and she snuggled up to him. Bridget received all of James' messages, but she didn't call him back right away she was too upset. When she did call him back, she left him a message saying they would talk when he got home the following week. When James came home he was so excited to see her, but she just sat stoic at the kitchen table. "Bridget, why are you mad at me? I didn't do anything wrong," He said trying to look her in the eye. "No you never do," She said standing up to go out the backdoor. They were all going to have a barbecue later that afternoon with the guys from the band. James followed her outside where Megan was playing in a sandbox with Dallas. James wrapped his arms around Bridget as she started the charcoal. "Babe please, I missed you don't treat me so cold," He said feeling hurt. Just then Megan noticed him and ran up wrapping her tiny arms around James' leg. "Daddy, daddy!" She screamed. "Hey baby girl, come here let me see my baby," He said as he lifted her up in his arms and gave her a huge squeeze. "Ok, Bridget. The guys and I talked, we won't be doing anymore full tours that last for long periods of time anymore. If we release more cd's we will try to keep most shows in the U.S where we can get home more," James said as he gently put Megan down on the grass. Bridget turned to look at him for a minute without saying a word, then she went back to lighting the charcoal. Just then Cullen, Marcus, Matt, Olivia, and Cindy walked out the backdoor. Megan pulled James by the hand over to the sandbox. Cindy came rushing up to Bridget, "Did you hear? They aren't going to be gone as much aren't you excited?" She asked her. "Yeah, if you can believe it. Besides I don't care about that much. What I care about is Jackie always around my husband," Bridget complained as she poked at the grill. Olivia came walking up to her and said, "You are going to really hate this then. I talked to Victoria this morning. Jackie is James' assistant at the office now." Bridget made a shocked face and shouted, "What!?" Bridget looked at James as he looked back at her. "He don't know yet," Olivia said. Bridget ran inside feeling enraged. James followed her inside. "What is wrong?" He asked confused. "I…. I can't take this anymore. I can't," She said crying hysterically. "Oh god what is it, baby? Tell me what it is!" He said panicking. "Jackie, that bitch. She is now your assistant according to Victoria," Bridget blurted out. James shook his head in disbelief, "Dammit! If you trust me honey, this won't be a problem. I don't want Jackie why can't you get that through your pretty head?" She started to get hysterical and shouted, "Because she wants you! I don't want her constantly throwing herself at you it makes me sick." Bridget started to hyperventilate. "Listen, calm down please. I promise you we will work through this. I will ask daddy if I can do most of my work from home I am sure he will let me. Just calm down for the baby," James begged her putting his arms around her. Bridget threw her arms around James. "I just love you so much and you are never here and when you are here it feels like you aren't here," She sobbed as he cradled her in his arms saying, "I know honey, that is going to change I am here I promise." He told her kissing her gently, "Let's go back out to the barbecue okay and we will get through this as long as we are strong together." When they came walking back outside Marcus came strolling up to Bridget as she wiped her eyes. "You know something I am going to kick your little skinny ass," He said as she looked at him confused. "Why, what did I do?" She asked still wiping her eyes. "Because, now my wife wants another baby. If I have twins again it is on your head," He said joking around with her. She laughed as she stared at him. "All kidding aside though, my brother adores you. You are everything to him. I know it may not seem that way, but it is true. You are his world," Marcus said trying to put her mind at ease as she looked on at James holding Megan tight in his arms. The summer was winding down. With all the tours James, Cullen and Marcus were always on there was not going to be a fight tournament that summer between the Mackenvoys and Hillenbrands. Joey, Walker and Billy were quiet upset by it. Joey found out Missy was expecting his first baby during the spring of the next year. By the end of July, Matt was already aware of his new addition coming along and now Olivia was pregnant. The summer was not easy for Bridget since she knew Jackie was in the office with James all day wearing her slutty outfits. So one day she decided she would surprise him by showing up at his office. He was surprised and excited to see her. She shut the door behind her and locked it after rudely telling Jackie to leave so she could have time alone with her husband. Walking over to him she sat on his lap and started passionately kissing him. Taking off her panties she grabbed his hand and made him touch her. He slipped his face under her skirt as she moaned in pleasure. It felt very erotic for him. They were on a high floor with a lot of windows, the only ones who would see them would be a helicopter. But, everyone outside of his office could hear them making love. An employee knocked on the door to ask if they were okay so they quit making love. But, Bridget promised later on that evening he would be satisfied. After she left, James was called to Colton's office. When he walked up to the office door Jackie came walking out giving him a nasty look. He entered the office and seen his father looking at him with a grumpy face while Rick stood by the window. "What the hell are you thinking son? This is a work place. Not a sex club," Colton said in an angry voice. "I am sorry daddy," James said looking down at the floor. Rick tried his best not to let the laughter slip out of his mouth. "Daddy, if you would let me see my wife more often this wouldn't happen. I miss her and I love her. Hell if you want to know the truth I didn't even get to finish because someone came knocking at the damn door!" James complained as Rick couldn't hold it back any longer he laughed hysterically while Colton gave him a crappy look. "Alright, I will let you out of here by 4:00pm from now on instead of 7:00pm that should help," Colton grumbled. James acted like a little kid who just got a new toy. "Now get the hell out of my office, and tuck in your shirt you look like hell," He said spinning around in his chair. As James left his office, Colton began to giggle right along with Rick as he shook his head. Bridget wasn't the only one who surprised her husband that day. Olivia got the idea to show up at Marcus' office. When she walked in she locked the door and turned to face him. He was on the phone and she walked slowly up to his desk unbuttoning her trench coat she had on. He continued to talk on the phone as she opened it. He stuttered when he seen she wasn't wearing anything under the trench coat. Getting down on her knees she crawled under his desk and began to unbutton his pants. When she took him in her mouth his voice went into a high pitched tone while she continued to suck hard and she began rubbing him up and down. Telling the person on the other end of the line he had to go, he hung up the phone and grabbed her arms. Bending her over his desk he held both of her arms behind her back as he licked around her butt cheeks with his tongue. Sinking his tongue inside her he moved it in and out repeatedly tickling her. Grabbing her hands rougher and holding tighter he shoved himself into her and began pumping up inside of her. The secretary sitting outside his office was an older lady. She began to blush as she heard both of them shout out in pleasure. Opening the door to his office to leave, Olivia looked over at the nice old lady and wished her a good day. When James returned home that night he brought pizza for dinner so Bridget wouldn't have to cook. Eyeing each other as they ate, Bridget could tell he wanted her since they didn't have time to finish earlier. After getting Megan to bed, Bridget could hear a huge thunderstorm in the background arriving. She turned off all the lights down stairs and wondered where James was. She was looking around the kitchen and made it to the back stair case when all the sudden he grabbed her. The lightning and thunder outside were becoming intense. He bent her over and began to slide into her a little forcefully. She liked his deep thrusts, but since he was so big it hurt. She pushed off of him and turned around to stare at him. She could only see his face with the flash of the lightning. She smiled and took off running whispering, "Catch me," She taunted him as he chased her through the hallway. She ran around the front stair case and into the dining room. He spun her around when he grabbed her and kissed her hard. Picking her up and pushing her against the wall he made love to her in a way that was powerful, but yet gentle as to not hurt the baby growing inside her belly. When they finished making love he walked her to their bedroom and laid her down on the bed. He gave her a soft sensual back massage as he said, "I have some good news for you, baby. Daddy is going to let me come home at 4:00 P.M instead of 7:00 P.M." Bridget turned around to look at him, "Are you serious? Thank god someone in your family finally has some good sense," She said laughing. Bridget felt at ease knowing she would finally have more of her husband's attention for once.

CHAPTER 17

When Victoria found out about the romp in the office she was disgusted with Bridget. And she definitely didn't want her spilling her poison onto Olivia or Emma with her antics. When Bridget was at the park with Megan the following morning, Victoria came to see her. She snuck up behind Bridget like a panther and said, "I hear you went to my husband's company yesterday." Bridget jerked around. "Who do you think you are doing such a low class thing?" Victoria asked looking her up and down. "I just wanted to be with my husband I don't get to see him much lately," Bridget tried to explain. But, Victoria interrupted her, "I don't care if you hadn't seen him for a year, you don't behave in such a disgusting way do you understand me? And for the record, James and Marcus are going to Haiti to help with the relief there. They will be staying a month." Bridget stood up and raised her voice, "What?! You can't do this to me!" As soon as she spoke Victoria smacked her across the face hard. Megan looked just in time to see. Bridget grabbed the side of her face stunned. "You don't call the shots in my family you little tramp. Soon my son will see you for what you are and I can't wait for that to happen," Victoria said as she stomped off before Bridget could say anything else. Bridget looked over at Megan with the sting still on her cheek. Victoria's plan was already in motion to get her out of her son's life. When Olivia found out Marcus had to leave for Haiti she was upset. She was all for him helping out in any way he could, but she knew this would take him away from her for yet another month while she was carrying his baby. She let it slip about the incident with Billy and Walker. Immediately Marcus called James and Cullen. All three guys planned on heading over to the bar the Hillenbrand guys hung out at. James asked Bridget why she hadn't told him what happened. She forgot with all of the issues with Jackie and the pregnancy. She didn't want James going to this bar and neither did Olivia so they followed along. When they walked into the bar all of the Hillenbrand boys were sitting at the bar along with their gaggle of friends. James called out to Billy, "Why the fuck did you try to run my wife down?" Billy and the rest of the guys turned around and stood up from their seats. Olivia and Bridget stood back watching in horror as yelling ensued. The song "Space Truckin" By Deep Purple began to play on the jukebox as a big brawl began. The bartender called for the cops as the girls yelled at their men to kick their asses. When Bridget noticed two guys holding James' arms while Billy beat him in the ribs hard, she became very pissed her off. She jumped over the bar and grabbed a broom to help her husband. Olivia figured if Bridget could help so should she. She grabbed a glass bashing it over a guy's head who was beating up Marcus. Marcus punched a tall man repeatedly and bashed his head up against the bar. A man pushed Olivia out of the way and picked Marcus up, hurling him over the bar into a huge mirror shattering it into pieces all over the floor. "Oh god, Marcus!" Olivia yelled as she grabbed a bar stool and hit it across the man's back knocking him to the floor. Bridget hit the fat man with her broom who was holding James by the arm, he turned around and pushed her down. James became enraged, he pushed through Billy knocking him to the floor. James hit the fat man with his shoulder violently sending the man to the floor as he shouted, "Don't push my pregnant wife you son of a bitch." He started beating on the man's head while Billy rushed over and hit James on the head and in the ribs repeatedly. Bridget hopped up and jumped on Billy's back trying to choke him into getting off of James. Cullen already had a pile of guys on the floor he had beaten senseless. Lifting many of them up over his head and body slamming them onto the floor. Nobody could get a hit on Cullen, except for Joey. He came sneaking up behind him and bashed him in the back of the head. Cullen turned around with an angry look on his face and said, "Really, mother fucker do you want a piece of me?" Cullen rushed up to Joey, Joey swung and missed as Cullen jumped back. Laughing, Cullen punched him square in the nose, sending Joey flying back into Walker. Joey landed on top of Walker as he shouted, "You son of a bitch!" Joey laid on the floor yelling in pain. Walker jumped up and started to rush at Cullen when Marcus ran into him like a bull knocking him to the floor. Olivia cheered in happiness, "Yes that's it baby! Kick his fucking ass!" She shouted jumping up and down. Marcus looked over at her, "Just stay out of the way Liv, I don't want you hurt!" Walker kicked the back of Marcus' calves causing him to fall onto the floor. Cullen seen Marcus fall and he rushed over. He picked Walker up by the neck, he head butted him hard and then tossed him across the room. Just then the cops came barging in asking them to stop what they were doing, holding up their guns at everyone. Bridget realized she still had her arms around Billy's neck. She looked down and let him go quickly like he was disgusting. She smacked the back of his head as she walked over to help James up. That night James had a collapsed lung and a few broken ribs so Bridget had to nurse him all night while he spit up blood in a pan. He didn't get much sleep, waking up coughing periodically. She thought during the night about how silly that whole fight was while she cradled James in her arms. But, all at the same time she felt a little bit of a rush helping her husband out. Although, he was upset with her for putting their baby at risk. That fight was caught on video camera for the world to see and America seemed to want more and more of these two families silliness. Bridget knew they weren't going to have a normal life anytime soon, if you could call it a normal life with the fighting let alone the cameras. For the next two months James, Cullen and Marcus all volunteered their help in Haiti. Bridget missed him so much, but she knew this was for a good cause. James would be back in time for the holidays. Her belly started to get bigger. She tried to feel at calm with her life. Billy noticed Bridget walking into a store while he sat out in his jeep with Walker. "Look at her. She wears a pregnant belly well don't you think?" Billy asked him in a serious way. Walker stared at Billy for a moment and then started to laugh hysterically. Billy looked at him fast getting very pissed off. "Now what the fuck are you laughing at?" Billy asked with an embarrassed tone. Walker just shook his head. "You are ate up. I have never seen you eye a woman like that before let alone a pregnant one," Walker said still laughing. Billy turned to look at Walker, "So?" Billy said looking back to see Bridget was gone. "I dare you to go in and talk to her. She went in the ice cream shop. Do it I dare you," Walker teased him. "Fine, I will I'm not afraid of anything," Billy said slamming his jeep door shut as Walker laughed. Bridget was at the counter getting Megan some ice cream. She turned around to see Billy standing in the doorway. "Oh god," She whispered to herself. "Come on sweetie, sit up here on the bench," She told Megan handing her the ice cream. Bridget sat down beside her daughter as Billy flopped down on the bench across the table from her. "Hi," He said staring at her with his big glassy blue eyes. She noticed he is a very handsome man with eyes that would melt any woman's heart. She could see how he was a ladies man. "What do you want, Billy Hillenbrand?" She asked. "Nothing, just wanted to see how you are doing," He said with a little smile. "And why do you care?" She asked him. He just looked deep into her eyes not answering. "It is taking you that long to think of an answer?" She said making fun of him. "No, I am just trying to figure out why James is such an idiot.

If I had a pretty wife like you here at home with my babies I couldn't leave your side," He flirted with her with his arms crossed on the table. She laughed out loud, "You? Having babies? Oh come on all you do is shoot guns with that crazy uncle of yours and try to sleep with women," She smirked. "Woe, wait now. First, there is nothing wrong with guns. People are the problem, not guns. And second, damn why do you put me down so much about the women thing? Maybe I just haven't found the right one yet who could steal my heart," He said with a serious tone raising his eyebrow. Bridget looked up from her ice cream asking, "You have a heart?" Billy was impressed with her wit. Most women flirt back with immediately, but she was different. Her stare was hypnotic to him. It felt deep when he would look at her and see her looking back. He shook his head for a minute wondering what was wrong with him. "Problem?" She asked wondering why he was acting so strange. "I got to go, but it was nice talking to you. I will see you later little fry," He said reaching over to rub Megan's hair. Megan took a big bite of her ice cream saying, "Bye, bye." Bridget watched Billy walk out of the store wondering what he was up to. When Billy made it back out to the jeep Walker asked, "Did you get in her panties?" Billy slammed the door uttering, "Shut up." As he started to pull out of the parking lot Walker laughed, "Struck out, loser!" The guys made it back home for the Halloween party. Bridget, Olivia and Cindy all found out they were going to be mothers to little boys. This was Matt and James first sons so they were over the moon excited. That winter they had promised to just do a few shows in other states, but that was okay with their wives. As long as they wouldn't be gone for weeks at a time. That February when Bridget's son was due it was to set off a chain of events that would change her life forever. Jon had visited her again while James was at a concert in California. When he went to leave her, he took a cute photo of them together to put on his Twitter page. Victoria had photos as well that she had secretly taken from his visit that previous May when Bridget had gotten pregnant. After Jon said his goodbyes to Bridget, Victoria showed up to have a talk with her. She brought with her the photos of her and Jon hugging. Bridget was shocked as she thumbed through the photos. "What is this? What are you trying to do?" She asked Victoria. "It is very simple my dear. I want you out of my son's life," Victoria said without skipping a beat. Bridget looked at her in disbelief. "What? I am getting ready to have his son, we have a daughter going on three years old. Why are you doing this?" Bridget asked her sadly. Victoria stood up from the table and said, "You were never good enough for my son. We both know that. I gave you a chance. You made a mockery of this family. I am ashamed to have you as a member of this family. There is a prestigious young lady from New York whom I would love my son to get to know. She is from a terrific wealthy family." As Victoria described this girl to her, she became upset and couldn't believe what she was hearing. "I would have thought you wanted him with Jackie," Bridget spoke up rudely. "My son, sadly, is blinded from the fact that Jackie is best for him. I do love her and wish she could be my daughter in law. And honestly that is still a possibility," Victoria snapped at her. Bridget sat shaking her head. She stood up to get the phone to call James. Victoria grabbed her arm violently and scowled, "You will leave my son alone. You will divorce him and let him live the life I had always wanted him to live." Bridget struggled trying to pull her arm away from Victoria. "I always get what I want. Look at my daughter, things worked out the way they were supposed to," Victoria said with the darkest eyes. Bridget stared into her eyes stunned, "Oh my god, did you have something to do with her miscarriage?" Bridget asked appalled. "Well whatever are you suggesting, my dear?" Victoria asked with a nasty look. All the sudden Bridget felt a cramping pain in her belly. Moaning loudly she grabbed her belly. "I need to call James, I think I am in labor," Bridget said in a weak breathy voice while Victoria looked like she could care less. She calmly grabbed her coat and pushed Bridget saying, "Let's go then." Victoria called Emma to babysit Megan. She drove Bridget to the hospital. On the way to the hospital she taunted her. "Soon my son is going to come to his senses and drop you like the trailer trash you are. And you can go back to Indiana where you will live your own life and James will live his. We can work something out with the kids," Victoria said giving her orders. Bridget tried to get her breath through the pain, "What is we? These are me and James' kids not yours." Arriving at the hospital, Victoria told Bridget she had contacted everyone. James was still in California, he couldn't be reached until after his show. Then he had to try to catch a flight to Tennessee. Bridget was in so much pain. She didn't have any pain management this time. She was in labor for 10 hours, when James finally made it to the hospital. The pain was so intense for her. She was sweating profusely, all the time begging for James. She didn't yell, she would just have a few tears. She wanted to show Colton and Rick that she was tough enough to be a member of this family. Maybe they could stop Victoria from doing what she was doing. She begged for James while she had the support of Olivia, but it wasn't the same. She wanted James there with her to hold her hand. Finally, he came running out of the elevator. "Where is my wife?" He yelled as he ran up to the front desk. Marcus, Cullen and Matt followed close behind. The doctor stopped him before he went into the room. "I am afraid there is a small problem. The baby is breech and it looks as though the placenta may rip if she tries to push him out," The doctor said in a matter of fact tone. James felt his heart sink as it pounded in his chest. "Well what does that mean?" He asked breathless from the run. "It means she needs a c-section. It is the best avenue to ensure your son and your wife make it through with no complications. She can be awake during it and you can be with her," The doctor explained as James absorbed what he told him. James took a deep breath and said, "Ok, let's do this." He calmly walked into the room to see Bridget first, he grabbed her hand and squeezed it. "Oh thank god James, it hurts so much. I just want it to stop," Bridget begged in a weak voice. "I know, baby, I know you are doing so good you are so strong. But, listen they have to take him out okay because there is a little problem. He is fine so don't worry," James tried to explain without worrying her. She became very concerned and started to cry. The doctor walked in to take her to surgery while James put on his scrubs he had to wear. The whole procedure took 15 minutes and before they knew it they heard their little boy cry with discontent. James and Bridget both cried as he kissed her lips and forehead. "Good job! You did it, Bridget. God look at him he is beautiful," James said with tears in his eyes. After he was cleaned up the nurse handed him to James. He walked out into the hall where everyone could see. "Hey everyone, meet Dylan Mackenvoy," James said with pride. Everyone cheered and patted him on the back with congratulations. James couldn't stop smiling. Bridget's delight didn't last long. She laid in the recovery room thinking about everything Victoria had said to her. Could this woman really cause her own daughter to miscarry? Or was she just trying to scare her into leaving James? What kind of an evil woman was this really?

CHAPTER 18

The first year after Dylan's birth, Victoria kept her tongue to herself about Bridget. Olivia went on to have a little boy named Hunter and Cindy had her little boy named Wyatt. James was so in love with his wife and his kids. This was by far the happiest time of his life. That would all come to an end soon. It all started at the February 2006 Valentine's Day dance both families held. Everyone was having a great time. Victoria sat on the top right side of the balcony with Colton, Rick and Mare while Packard, Lisa and Jack sat on the left side of the balcony. The song "Eyes Without A Face" By Billy Idol blared as Victoria fidget in her seat. She continually kept staring at the front door to the gym. Colton noticed her fidgeting. "Darling, what is wrong with you? Expecting someone are we?" He asked as she looked at Colton smiling. When Victoria turned to look back at the door when in she walked, the red haired bombshell from New York. She strolled in the front door looking around when she noticed Victoria up on the balcony. James, Bridget, Olivia, Marcus and Cullen all sat with their backs to the front door not noticing her walking in. But across the gym sitting at his table Billy did. He looked over at Joey and said, "Look at this hottie walking in." Joey looked her way. "She's okay, looks a little preppy," Joey grumbled. Joey and Missy were doing well, although not married. She was home with their little boy, Noah, who was sick. Noah was born just two months after Dylan the previous year. Walker came strolling up behind Billy and Joey. "Wow, I would love to get a hold of that!" Walker said licking his lips. Billy stared at this red haired beauty walking up to the staircase that led to the balcony. She passed James and Bridget glancing quickly their way. Billy watched her the whole time when all the sudden Bridget caught his eye. Once he began to stare at her, he couldn't turn away his eyes. Victoria walked down the stairs to greet the mysterious lady who intruded on their party. Smiling, Victoria gave her a big hug and walked her over to meet James. "This is my youngest son, James. James, this is Amy Winters from New York. Her father is CEO at a very prestigious company that has offices all over the world." Victoria said proudly giving Bridget a nasty glare. James stood up holding out his hand to shake Amy's and said, "Hello it is nice to meet you. This is my wife Bridget." As Bridget stood up to shake her hand Victoria rolled her eyes. Billy was watching the whole time. "Hi, it is nice to meet you," Bridget said with a small handshake. Amy feeling a little uncomfortable flipped her hair over her shoulder as Victoria talked more about her family. Bridget felt completely left out and sick to her stomach. Here was the woman Victoria was hoping would replace her. Bridget sat for about five minutes while James stood and talked to Amy. Olivia looked over at Bridget and reached over to touch her hand. "I need to go to the restroom," Bridget said hopping up, rushing out of the gym. Victoria gave a huge smile as she watched her run out. Billy stood up and walked out of the gym to see Bridget standing by the bathroom wiping her eyes. He walked up to her slowly and said, "Hello lady, are you okay?" She looked over at him and stared for a moment. "I will be okay, I am just not feeling too well," She said taking a breath. Billy shook his head in a yes motion and stared down at the floor. "James Mackenvoy is an idiot," He said looking back up at her. She just stared back into his beautiful blue eyes. "Is he? Maybe he was an idiot for marrying me," She said as she walked by Billy and back to the gym. Billy stayed behind wondering how James could be so insensitive. When Bridget went back into the gym, James was sitting back down talking to Marcus. Bridget didn't say a word about the situation, but Victoria felt confident she had done her job well. Indeed, James seemed to be very interested in the conversation with Amy. For the next month Bridget hid her hurt, but little did she know Victoria had another trick up her sleeve to seal the deal of getting her out of James life. While James was at work Victoria paid him a little visit. "Hello my boy, how is your day going?" She asked him sitting down across from him. "I'm good momma, what did I do to deserve a visit today?" He asked as she smiled for a moment and then said, "Son, I need to talk to you about something that will be very difficult for you to comprehend, but you need to hear me out." James stared at her anxiously waiting to hear what she had to say. Pulling out a large manila envelope she laid it down in front of him. "This was caught when you were on tour right before Bridget became pregnant with Dylan," Victoria said without any regrets of what she was about to do to her son's life. James looked up at her confused and afraid to open the envelope. He slowly opened the envelope and pulled out photos of Jon and Bridget hugging. He thumbed through the photos seeing what could be only described as friends meeting up for a visit. When he got to the last page, it was Jon kissing Bridget on the cheek. The photo was far away so he couldn't really see too well. It looked like he was kissing her on the cheek, but to him what he seen was Jon kissing his wife on the lips. Then, Victoria pulled out a photo that Jon had taken himself that he had put on twitter of himself and Bridget. There she was holding her pregnant belly with her hand and standing beside Jon sitting in a chair making a silly face. Bridget had a big smile on her face in the photo. "I am sorry to have to show you these, but I knew you needed to see this. I think it is best for you to have a paternity test," Victoria callously said. James looked up at her with tears in his eyes. "You don't think my son is really my son?" He said with a crack in his voice. "I am just saying, look at these photos. It is around the same time of her pregnancy. And I am sorry to say, Dylan has dark brown hair. Look at Jon, he does favor him," Victoria said furthering her suspicion. Slamming down his fist on the table and said, "Dammit momma, he is my son. He looks like me just like Megan does!" He raised his voice. "I am not so certain. I can see the resemblance of Jon in his face and hair," She smirked. Agitated, James jumped up from his seat grabbing the photos as he began to storm out of the office. "I am going home!" He said slamming the door behind him. Victoria just sat in her seat feeling relieved and happy with the chaos she was causing. Slowing she stood up and walked to Colton's office to see how her husband's day was going. She didn't explain her visit to James, just that he had to go home and wouldn't be back in the office that day. Colton never agreed with Victoria's meddling, but he also didn't like drama so he tended to stay out of it. Colton had no idea what Victoria was up to. Bridget was playing music and singing to Dylan in his high chair as Megan danced around the kitchen. She felt good that day regardless of what feelings she had been burying lately. Stirring the cookie dough in the bowl she heard a huge slam of the door. James came stomping into the kitchen. Megan seen him and ran up to him happily jumping up into his arms screaming, "Daddy!" Picking her up and squeezing her he looked over at Dylan sitting in his high chair. Bridget stared at James with a confused face. Obviously he was very upset. "Is everything okay, sweetie?" She asked nervously as to what had just happened. Rubbing Megan's back for a second he kissed her and said, "Come on baby girl, you and little D are going to go to the living room to watch cartoons. Momma and I have to talk." Bridget was really nervous now. She picked up Dylan and followed James into the living room to put him in his playpen while James turned on cartoons. Turning the volume very high he looked over at Bridget and said, "Get into the kitchen right now." She turned and started to walk down the hallway. "What….. what the hell is your problem?" She asked having no idea what he was so upset about. "Is he mine?" He asked as she looked at him confused. "Is who yours, what are you talking about?" She asked him getting angry. He became even angrier and shouted, "Dylan! Is Dylan my boy?" Aghast Bridget looked back at him feeling enraged. "How can you ask me something like that? Of course he is yours. I have never been unfaithful to you a day in my life!" She began to raise her voice in frustration. "Look at his hair, Bridget. Look how dark his hair is, my hair isn't like that and yours isn't like that!" James shouted as she stared at the floor in disbelief. "Dylan has dark hair just like the rest of your family does. Megan has your hair color, but Dylan apparently took after your sickening mother," She said with tears in her eyes. James paced around the kitchen floor and then he said, "I want you to prove it." She looked back up at him confused and asked, "Prove it?" He shook his head in a yes motion. "Do a paternity test," He said staring her down. Irate Bridget began to raise her voice again, "This is your mother. I can't believe you are letting her do this to us. I have always been faithful to you, James. If anyone should ever have to worry it should have been me, not you. If you loved me, I mean truly loved me then you would know that Dylan is your son. I am asking you to trust me, when have I ever made you not feel as though you couldn't trust me? You knew about Jon visiting me that day. And you know there is nothing going on between me and Jon. He is happily in a relationship with someone two times better looking than me. He is my friend and that is all. How would you feel if I kept accusing you of fucking Jackie?" James looked at her for a minute feeling a little foolish in a way. Bridget walked up to James grabbing his face in her hands. "I love you, James, so much. Don't let your momma do this. You know she doesn't like me. I love you and I would never betray you in that way, ever. That little boy is 100% yours. Will you please just let this go? If you truly love me and trust me, then you don't need a paternity test," She whispered while kissing him, he wrapped his arms around her. He began to cry, "I am so confused, baby, I don't know what to think anymore. Momma has always been telling me stuff about you over the years." Bridget jumped back and asked, "Like what?" She let go of James' shoulders. He started to explain to her, "Just stupid stuff, like always telling me you are always sneaking off places when I am working…." Bridget interrupted, "That is a damn lie!" He just looked at her. "Please, James just trust me. Prove to your momma she can't do this to us. Prove to her that you trust me completely by telling her she can go to hell and no paternity test." He thought for a moment and then looking up he said, "You are right you haven't done anything for me not to trust you. You don't deserve to be treated this way. I will give you the benefit of the doubt, no paternity test." She hugged him tightly as he stared off wondering if he could really trust Bridget completely. Things were looking up for Victoria. She had already set Emma up with a very rich man named Jeremy and she was now expecting her first daughter. Jeremy and Emma had married over the winter in a quick ceremony. And, now she almost had Bridget out of her son's life. A week had passed since the fight with Bridget, but Victoria wasn't finished working on James. She made it known around town that Dylan may not be her grandson. Her goal was to humiliate Bridget and make James out to be an innocent young man who was hurt by his cheating wife. This would leave the door open for him to move on with Amy no matter if he had a family. Billy heard the talk around town. Bridget tried her best to ignore it. She figured if James loved and trusted her that was all that mattered. Billy seen Bridget's car parked at the café and he felt as though he had to stop to see her. When he walked into the building he seen her sitting at a table with Megan and cradling Dylan in her arms as she stood up to get ready to leave. Billy walked up to her smiling slyly. "Hello there, my lady," He said as she looked him in the face with a small smile. "Hello how are you, Billy?" "Never mind how I am, how are you?" She thought as she reached to grab her purse and she said, "I am great, I couldn't be better." Billy feeling a bit surprised asked, "Really? I would have thought you would be going insane with all the talk." Bridget didn't say a word at first and stared at his blue eyes. "I don't care what people in this town say about me. James knows who I am and the truth that is all that matters to me," she said. Billy leaned in getting up close to Dylan's face. "Hmmm, yep I can see it. He is definitely a Mackenvoy. He reeks of James that is for sure," Billy said smiling as he walked off. Bridget stood a little stunned. Why didn't Billy try his usual tricks? He could have easily used this to his advantage to drive her crazy, but he didn't. She was impressed with how he treated her in that moment. She wanted to call out to thank him, but he was already gone.

CHAPTER 19

Victoria enjoyed her time with Megan and Dylan. She knew Dylan was James' son, but she just couldn't help it. She had to get this girl out of her family. Amy was very interested in James and she was more than willing to have more kids with him. Amy would just sit back, waiting to see if James would ever leave Bridget. Victoria made Amy believe as well that Bridget had cheated on James repeatedly with Jon Spencer. Amy was a kind soul and not the type who would bust up a marriage. She wore very conservative clothes and had perfect hair and makeup at all times. She was an improvement on Jackie. She didn't have anything fake on her. She didn't have to. She was naturally gorgeous with her bright auburn hair and big blue eyes. Bridget felt a different kind of jealousy for Amy. She was perfect in every way, including personality. It made her sad to feel as though maybe James did deserve someone as special as Amy was. Why was he wasting his life with her? Maybe Victoria was right and James was made for so much more. Victoria was babysitting Megan and Dylan while Bridget had her yearly checkup. James was at work as he usually was at 2:00pm on a Thursday. On her way to Victoria's to pick up the kids, her phone rang. Answering it through sync she heard Jon's voice come over the speakers, "Hey there girl, I just thought I would let you know I got the results back. Not like it mattered we both knew the truth right?" Jon laughed as Bridget became confused. "Jon, what are you talking about?" She asked as she giggled. He was quiet for a moment. "The paternity test. The results were just sent to me I assumed you and James got yours too?" He said confused. She sat looking out the windshield in a state of shock. "We didn't do any paternity test, James knows we weren't messing around with each other he promised me no test," She said starting to pause for a time. "Bridget, I had to do the paternity test for Dylan. James didn't tell you?" Jon asked surprised. Sick to her stomach to the point of wanting to vomit, Bridget pulled the car over. "No….. Jon, he didn't tell me. I have to go now. Thanks for letting me know," Bridget said stunned. "Are you going to be okay?" Jon asked her. "Yes, bye my friend," She said hanging up the line. All the sudden she began to break down in loud sobs, she punched the steering wheel screaming at the top of her lungs. Grabbing her hair on the sides of her head she thought to herself. This is not happening, he did it. He went behind her back and did it. Throwing her car into gear she rushed to Victoria's house. Beating on the door, Victoria opened it calmly and said, "Hello dear….." Before she could finish her sentence Bridget yelled at her, "Get my kids you bitch! I am not coming in your shitty house just give me my kids!" Victoria stared at her in an evil way and said, "There is no need to use that kind of language." Walking away from the door she got the kids and brought them to the door. Yanking Dylan out of Victoria's hands and leading Megan to the car she turned to Victoria, "You stay the hell away from me and my babies you psycho." She jumped in her car and sped away. Megan was watching Bridget cry with a sad look to her face. "Awe, momma, why you sad. Do you miss daddy? I miss daddy," She said in a whiney voice. When Bridget heard her daughter talk she began to cry hysterically again. She knew her marriage was over. When James came home from work that night, Bridget already had her bags packed. He came in looking at them lying on the floor confused and he said, "Babe, what's going on?" She came walking up to the bags. "Don't give me that shit," she said with her eyes still red and puffy from the constant crying. "What are you talking about?" He asked trying to grab her arms. "Don't touch me!" She yelled jerking away from him, "I think it is best if we separate. I am going to see Marcus now, he will file the legal separation documents tomorrow. You will have your space to go for Amy or Jackie or whoever your little heart desires." Standing in disbelief he kept trying to grab Bridget. "I don't understand, baby, talk to me," He shouted nervously as she stopped grabbing at the bags and looked at him. "You know that is the scariest part of it all. You can lie to me and have a paternity test behind my back with your mother and not feel a twinge of guilt for it." She said as his heart fell to his toes. He looked her deep in the eyes and tears began to wail up in his eyes. "Baby, I am sorry, please I know Dylan is mine now. Momma can just be so damn manipulating. I promise nothing like this will ever happen again," He said feeling it all slip away. "Your right, it won't," She said opening the front door holding her bags. "I will leave the kids with you for the night. I am going to rent a small house in town. I just think this is best," She said shutting the door behind her. James slid down to the floor and began to cry very hard. Megan came walking up to him and hopped into his lap. "You sad because momma is sad?" She asked him looking up in James' watery eyes. "It will be okay baby girl, momma won't be gone long I promise," He said hugging her tightly as he vowed to win Bridget back. He refused to let this be the end. On the way to Marcus' office she knew it was going to be hard to file separation papers. She couldn't bring herself to file divorce papers just yet. Marcus tried his best to talk her out of the legal separation. "Look, momma can be very persuasive. She does these things because she wants things the way she wants them," Marcus started to say but Bridget interrupted him and said, "James is a grown man. He can make his own decisions. He chose to go behind my back, do a paternity test and believe all her lies about me. I just can't do this anymore. Not right now. I think I need to let James find out what he needs in his life. I need to step back and give him space. And I need space. This time I have spent in this family has consumed me. It has eaten me up over the years and I just can't take it anymore. I can't pretend to be this perfect woman for him to make your mom happy. I am just exhausted, Mark, I am exhausted. Just file those papers." The papers were filed for legal separation and once again it was in all the tabloid magazines. Jon was put in the middle making it seem as though he broke up James Mackenvoy's marriage, the awesome rock star. It was a hit to Jon's popularity as an actor. Gossip in the celebrity world can be a bear and ruin lives and careers. Bridget apologized for causing strife to Jon's life. In May 2006, Bridget had an offer from a survivor type of show to join the cast for the following autumn show. She took the offer. It was her chance to prove to herself that she was cunning enough to figure things out and beat a lot of other sly people. The million dollars wasn't what Bridget was after, it was to prove to herself she was strong. It would be a huge challenge, but worth it to her in the long run. It would also get her out of this town for a month and a half. She would miss her babies in that amount of time, but it wouldn't last forever and maybe she would accomplish something to make her kids proud. When she arrived by helicopter to her location on the beach, she could feel the nerves in her stomach. She not only had to prove to herself she was worth something, but now she had to prove to the world. The cameras would be rolling for the whole world to watch her succeed or fail. Standing in the sand listening to the rules of the game everyone is stunned to find another group of people joining the cast. When Bridget noticed who was looking back at her she shook her head thinking why me. It was none other than Billy Hillenbrand. He just smiled back at her in a way where she felt uncomfortable. She knew he was relentless and nobody could beat Billy. He was good at manipulation, better than Victoria, and his strength could be reckoned with. Her hopes of winning the million dollars was shattered. After the drawing she found out she is stuck in the same tribe as Billy. She couldn't believe her luck. During the first two weeks on the island with Billy, she stayed away from him if at all possible. A lot of the women on the tribe adored Billy. He did exactly what he had always done, wrapped women around his finger. But, Bridget wasn't one of them. She stayed to her own alliance while he stayed to his. There were a few rumblings that Bridget's name was on the chopping block. She knew not many people liked her although she never understood why. She was in a great alliance with a gay man named, Clive. He was a fantastic man who could make her laugh at the top of her lungs. Walking to talk strategy with Clive, she knew she would have to work this to her favor. She couldn't lose this game at any cost. Billy didn't have anything at all against gay people, however he never understood the desire for it. He was fine being friends with gay men, as long as they knew he was completely straight. He was kind of a homophobe. At one point while Bridget was sunning herself by a small pool of water, Billy came over to visit. He made a few remarks referring to Clive and his sexual preference. Bridget just stared at Billy stunned and asked, "What the fuck is wrong with you?" Billy just laughed as she hopped up to walk away. Billy was also known to have had a few girls in the tribe perform oral sex on him. He was never caught doing this, it was just rumor around the camp. Most of the guys on the tribe were too afraid to stab Billy in the back. Many of the cast knew all about the Hillenbrand family along with Bridget and the Mackenvoys. Nobody said much to any of them about their show or families. Bridget was sitting by the camp talking to a few of the other ladies in the tribe when Billy was cooling off in the ocean. Clive floated over to Billy and let him know how handsome and sexy he thought he was along with some other things. Billy had his face half under the water up to his nose and all you could see was his eyes go from looking at Clive to panning over to the girls by the camp. Bridget began to giggle when she realized her plan was in full force. Billy hopped up out of the water and walked by the camp looking over at Bridget with a sour face. She kept a serious look on her face like she knew nothing about what was said in the water. Billy was rattled and that is what she wanted. All of the challenges were brutal for Bridget, but she and Billy came through them perfectly. Even Colton and Packard who watched the show that following fall were impressed with her strength emotionally and physically. Billy also noticed it. In fact, he tried to keep her name out of the list of being kicked off the island. She secretly had done the same for Billy. She knew he was a strong smart player and she needed him to get to the end. Sleeping at the camp was rough. It would get stormy and cold at times and Bridget hated the cold. Everyone would typically huddle up to keep warm, but there were always two girls surrounding Billy. The tribe was shrinking from all the people being kicked off, but he still had the two girls who were interested in him constantly fawning all over him. On one particular night Billy noticed Bridget was cold and shaking. He took his shirt off and laid it on her. She jumped startled turning to look at him. "Why did you give me this?" She asked. "I see your cold go ahead I don't need it. I don't get cold much," He whispered. She thanked him as she turned her back to him to fall asleep. The next morning when everyone woke up, they noticed how Billy had his arms completely wrapped around Bridget. He was huddled over her in a way that all you could see was a little bit of her face through his blonde bangs laying on her cheek. When she awoke to the sound of laughter she realized Billy's arms draped over her. Pushing his arms away, she raised up and sleepy eyed laid his shirt down beside him. Walking away she went to get a drink and she had to relieve herself. Coming up behind her was another kind girl from the tribe. "Billy is really sexy isn't he in a Brad Pitt sort of way?" She asked. Bridget jumped and said, "Oh hey, Lara, I won't lie he is hot, but not my type I am married." Lara stared at her with a smile and asked, "You are separated aren't you?" Embarrassed Bridget just walked away. It was close to the end of the competition, there were still a few weeks to go. Everyone was starving. During a challenge many of the tribe members could buy food or use their money for a clue. Bridget decided she would hold out for the clue. When a bowl of peanut butter came into play it was so hard for Bridget to not buy it. She loved peanut butter and she could literally feel her stomach eating itself. Her mouth watered profusely. When all the sudden Billy raised his hand to buy the peanut butter. Walking up to get his prize he was told to eat what he could for the next two minutes and then walk back to his seat, but he had to leave the bowl of peanut butter behind. He gobbled down what peanut butter he could covering his hands in globs of peanut butter. Bridget watched dying to have some for herself. Billy was told to go back to his seat and the next item was up for bids. Bridget got what she was after, a clue. Walking back to her seat with the clue she could see Billy still trying to eat some of the peanut butter out of his hands. Suddenly, the guy calling the shots told Billy he could pick one person to share the peanut butter with that was left on his hands. He looked down at Bridget and mentioned her while the two girls who were obviously involved with him looked stunned. Bridget didn't have to think twice, she ran up to sit next to Billy. Grabbing his right hand she began licking the palm of his hand and sucking the peanut butter off his fingers while Billy sat staring at her with his mouth gaped open. She was so hungry she didn't care what it looked like to everyone. Billy himself became so aroused by this he couldn't stop thinking about it over the next several days. The whole time Bridget was away on the island, James was being pushed together with Amy. She would visit him often at his house. His mother was pulling all the strings. Megan asked Amy many times. "Where is my momma? You aren't my momma, why are you here?" Amy would never know what to say. Hurling her cereal at Amy's face, Megan began to scream, "Where's my momma?" James came walking into the room and he said, "Hey, hey what are you doing? You aren't supposed to be mean to daddy's friends." Picking Megan up and cradling her in his arms he looked at Amy and apologized. Megan always was the type of kid who would lose her temper and hit her cousins on the head in frustration. Dylan was more laid back. James looked at Amy and said, "I am going to get my wife back. This isn't over. I am not going to lose her over some silly mistake I made." Amy stared at him not knowing what to say. "My momma has interfered for the last time in my marriage. I love my wife so much. For the past 5 years we haven't been able to have a proper husband and wife relationship. That ends when she gets home. I'm going to romance the panties off my wife and show her how much I love her, I promise you that," He said as he walked away with Megan in his arms. When James turned to walk away with Megan she stuck her tongue out rudely at Amy. Amy looked down at Dylan and gave him a little smile. He smiled back with a big cheesy grin. Nothing inappropriate happened with James and Amy. His mind and heart was still with Bridget and when he found out Billy was stuck on this island with her he was disgusted and constantly worried about his wife. It was down to the wire and one of the final challenges as a tribe had Billy and Bridget working together. She was afraid of heights, but in the challenge she had to stand on Billy's shoulders to stack items on top of one another to make a tower without it falling in the wind. She begged Billy before she stepped up on his shoulders to please not drop her. She was so terrified she had to completely put her trust in him. He was amazingly cool and calm. He didn't move an inch the whole time Bridget was teetering on his shoulders. When they won the challenge he put her down gently as she looked into his eyes for a minute. The rough time on the island was soon over. It was down to the last three people standing, among the three was Billy and Bridget. Also in the final three was one of the girls who had an affair going on with Billy. Bridget had suspicions that he carried his little friend to the final three because he liked her so much.

CHAPTER 20

It was a hot humid August morning. On her flight home, Bridget was so nervous to find out if she had won the contest. She had a feeling it would either be herself or Billy. She missed her babies so much. She couldn't wait to get home to them. She thought of them every night out on that island. She even found herself talking to Billy about her kids. She is so proud of them she would tell anyone who would sit long enough to listen. She also thought about James, but inside her heart felt as though it was exploding. How could he hurt her so much? How could he not trust or love her like she believed he did for six years? When she drove home to town she couldn't wait to grab those babies up in her arms. It was mid-morning, pulling into the driveway she felt nervous. When she started to walk up to the door she could hear Megan screaming. Bridget ran into the house screaming, "James?" She looked around the house frantically when James came running in the back door with Megan in his arms. "Oh, Bridget you scared me," He said handing Megan over to her. "Momma, momma!" Megan screamed at the top of her lung, "Dallas don't move." Bridget looked at James. He shook his head and whispered that Dallas had died over night in the back yard. He was old and sick. They knew he wouldn't live too long, but Dallas lived two years longer than he was supposed to. Bridget began to cry as she held Megan in her arms, suddenly she heard Dylan start to cry up in his crib. She rushed up there to hold him too. She was so happy to see her babies, but she had no idea the reunion would be this way. James walked outside and stood over Dallas for a few minutes. He went to the back of the yard and began to dig the hole for Dallas' grave. Bridget looked out her master bedroom window watching James did the hole as the kids lay down on her bed. Dylan was still too young to understand, but Megan knew something was wrong with her doggy, she adored him. Megan dozed off to sleep on the master bed, so Bridget grabbed Dylan up in her arms and walked him downstairs to the living room. She heard the back door open as she turned Dylan on cartoons. James got himself a cold beer out of the refrigerator and sat down at the kitchen table with his back to the hallway. Bridget looked down the hallway and seen him rubbing his face and making weeping sounds. She slowly walked up to him and started to rub his back and then she moved her hands up to the back of his head and rubbed it affectionately. "I miss you, Bridget," He said in a crackling voice choking back tears. "You missed our anniversary," He said as she moved over to sit down in the chair right beside him. "Yes I had to do the contest, but it is no different than all those anniversaries you have missed because of your tours," She said sadly as he looked at her with tears in his eyes. "In our whole marriage, we have had one honeymoon and went one place for our anniversary. I stayed here and took care of Megan and also your son, Dylan," She said wanting to get the point across how it stung what he did with the paternity of their little boy. "I can see where things were so hard for you. You deserved so much better than me, Bridget," He said as he reached over to grab her hand in his. "Will you please come home? Stop this ridiculous separation. I want to hold my wife, I want to kiss you and make you feel what is in my heart. Do you hear me? I love you, Bridget. More than I love my own life. Let us raise our kids together and have more…." As he started to finish the sentence she stood up and said, "I can't, not now. It is too hard." She started to cry when he grabbed her by the arm. "Bridget, please come back to me," He said as he came up to her grabbing her face and passionately kissing her. She couldn't stop herself from kissing him back. "Oh, James, I love you so much," She said grabbing his face and looking him in his beautiful brown eyes. Suddenly, James dropped to his knees and began to pull her jeans down. Her panties were still on when James laid his nose against her, smelling her through her panties. "God, I missed you so much," He said pulling down her panties quickly and licking her all over. Sinking his tongue deep inside her she tried not to make too much noise as to not to disturb Dylan in his playpen. Standing up he unzipped his pants real fast and shoved himself up inside her. Pumping her up against the wall hard she couldn't help but make noise from the sheer largeness of him. He moaned as he kissed her neck repeatedly. Digging her nails into his back as he felt himself release inside of her. All the sudden they heard Megan behind them say, "Daddy, are you hurting momma?" He hurried up and zipped his pants up with his back to Megan. "No, honey daddy isn't hurting momma," Bridget said as she ran over pulling back on her pants. She grabbed Megan up in her arms hugging her and said, "Momma and daddy were just hugging and kissing because we missed each other so much." Megan looked at her for a moment. "Oh," She said not really understanding. James phone rang while Bridget was talking to Megan. He looked at the phone to see it was Amy. He laid the phone down on the table and didn't answer it. Bridget stood up and asked, "Who was that?" James looked at her for a minute and said, "Nobody important. You and my kids are what is important." He reached out to grab her as she held Megan. "So, what do you say will you come back home?" He asked her looking her deep in the eyes. Bridget looked at Megan and gave her a smile. "Can we talk about this later?" She asked James. "Sure, if you want to," He said feeling disappointed, "By the way, I heard you weren't alone over on that island." Bridget looked at him quickly, "Oh really?" He shook his head yes and said, "Yeah dumbass Joey is all excited about his little brother winning the title and the million." Bridget gave a little smirk, "Jerks, it isn't like they need the money they are rich," She said putting Megan down. "You don't either, baby, you have me," James said looking at her intensely. Bridget stared at him not knowing what to say. James phone rang again and he kept staring at Bridget. She shuffled past him and said, "Aren't you going to get that?" As she started to grab his phone he shouted, "Bridget, wait!" She looked at him quickly. "Why? It's Olivia, or was you expecting someone else?" She asked quizzically. James took the phone and answered it. Bridget all the sudden felt that ugly non trusting feeling rising in her stomach again. "Hey, baby, Liv wants to talk to you," James said handing her the phone. She took the phone from James' hand and listened to all she had to say. Olivia was all excited Bridget was back home. She also tried to talk her into moving back in with James. Olivia gave her the news from Joey expecting his second child to her and Marcus getting matching tattoos on their lower belly's bearing each other's names. Bridget reminded her that she pretty much cursed herself by doing that. She also told her that Cindy and Matt seemed to be doing very well lately. Of course, they were doing better on the account of the band hadn't released any new albums yet so no tour dates had been made. Cindy felt she needed her husband and when he was away she missed him so much she felt like she would fall apart. Bridget spent the night with James, but knew this didn't mean they were back together. It was going to take a lot of work on his part to make her believe he was sorry. She also needed to know that he learned his lesson. One night Bridget came walking into the living room to see James laid back in his recliner sound asleep. Megan was also asleep laying belly down on his chest. It was one of the sweetest things she had ever seen. The next morning he had to go to work, but Bridget stayed at the house with the kids instead of taking them to her rental house. James was over the moon happy when he left the house that morning. It would be short lived. Victoria showed up to speak to Bridget. Reluctantly letting her in the house, Bridget wasn't pleasant with her. She despised this evil woman who was trying her best to ruin her marriage. "So, are you back?" Victoria asked Bridget rudely. "Not that it is any of your business," Bridget snapped back. Victoria laughed, "You realize the whole time you were gone my son was not alone?" Bridget looked at her with a puzzled look. "What kind of shit are you trying to make up now?" Bridget asked her, "You really think I am going to believe anything you have to say?" Victoria shrugged, "You can believe what you want, my dear. But, the fact is Amy was very comforting to my son every night she stayed here." Victoria stopped speaking for a moment to look at Bridget, "Oh yes, you heard me right. She stayed here for several nights when you rudely left my son to meander with Billy Hillenbrand on an island." Bridget knew she would use what she had to. "I didn't know Billy would be there," Bridget snapped. Victoria turned around quickly, "You are trying to tell me when that silly show airs in September we aren't going to see anything questionable? Let's face it, he is a disgusting dog and you, well you are a worthless trailer trash rat." Bridget started to get teary eyed as Victoria insulted her and it started to sink in about James. She remembered the phone call he wouldn't answer. After hugging her grandkids, Victoria walked up to Bridget, "I hope you will be smart and finish the divorce. The legal separation is just buying you time. I could have Marcus draw up the papers for you." Bridget didn't say a word as Victoria slithered out the door. Victoria picked up on Bridget's uneasiness when she asked her about the show being aired in September. She set out looking for Billy. She checked all his usual hang outs, but couldn't find him. She decided to ask one of his drinking buddies at the bar down town. He had red hair and very skinny, not a very attractive man. His name was Rodney. He was more than willing to give Victoria Billy's itinerary. Rodney could use the money, and Victoria would easily pay him off to do dirty jobs for her. He told her Billy was working on a house with his brother on the east side of town. She immediately drove over to see him. When she walked in she looked around the home when Joey seen her. He threw his arms up in front of his face shouting, "Oh my god, the angel of darkness is here, no go away!" He laughed loudly as Victoria nastily lashed out, "Shut up you pathetic worm, where is your brother?" Joey looked around for a minute and said, "I don't know, what is worth to you?" She looked him up and down and said, "You are disgusting." After she finished her sentence she heard Billy's voice behind her. "Why the hell do you want to see me?" She spun around with a smile on her face. "Billy," She said strolling up to him, "Could I speak to you in private please?" Billy looked over at Joey, Joey just shrugged and started to walk out of the half-finished house. "This house is quaint," She said pretending to care. "It is a habitat for humanity house. We do what we can," Billy said staring at her while she had her back to him. "Now, what the hell do you want?" He asked inpatient. She turned around and started to walk up to him speaking slyly, "I have a proposition for you." "Oh?" He asked intrigued. "My son is no longer in love with Bridget and she is going to need a distraction so she don't embarrass herself in the process of their divorce. I am sure you heard, they are legally separated?" Victoria said as he nodded. "So what are you wanting me to do? I am not into doing any favors for Mackenvoys, especially the likes of James," He asked her hatefully. "Do what you normally do. She would slip into bed with you in no time I am sure," Victoria sneered. "Oh, you want me to fuck her?!" Billy raised his voice shocked. "Don't use that foul language with me. You and Bridget are one in the same. You deserve each other," She said acting as though she was disgusted. Billy looked off for a moment and said, "What if I don't want to do this? What if I think she is a nice person and she shouldn't be treated that way?" Victoria looked at him with surprise. "Billy Hillenbrand caring about a woman's feelings?" He angrily interrupted, "You know I am getting sick and tired of hearing that shit. I have more of a heart than a mean old bitch like you does." She just smiled as she turned to leave, "I will keep in touch. Think about what I said." Billy thought for a while about what Victoria had said. He felt something whenever he thought of Bridget, but he wasn't sure what it was. It definitely wasn't just him wanting to get laid. But, he did know she seemed like a nice person and he couldn't stand the thought of her being tortured by Victoria or James for that matter. He also knew deep down that she beat him at the game on the island. He wouldn't admit that one, but he just knew. She played a good game and she deserved to win. He knew what house Bridget was renting so he thought he would take a ride over to see her. When he got there she wasn't home, so he sat in her driveway for a little bit before deciding to grab a quick drink. When James returned home from work Bridget was waiting to talk with him about what his mother told her. Sadly, she had asked Megan earlier that day if there was any other woman staying there while she was gone. Megan confirmed her biggest fear. Sitting James' supper down on the table she sat directly across from him. She thought about what Megan had said as she watched him eat. "James, can I ask you something?" She asked him while he took a few bites of his food. He looked up at her, "You can ask me anything you want." She looked down at her hands and said, "Okay, was Amy here while I was gone and did she spend the night?" James slowly raised his fork to his mouth biting the food off and sat the fork back down. "Yes she was and yes she spent the night. But, nothing happened I swear to you. She was just helping out with the kids because I really didn't know what I was doing where they were concerned," He said while Bridget rolled her eyes frustrated. "Oh please, she has no kids how the hell could she help!?" Bridget asked angrily, "Please don't get mad about this. I have a right to be mad, too! You file for separation and then you go spend almost two months on an island with Billy Hillenbrand!" James yelled back. "Don't try to make that sound like I was doing something wrong, James, you are the one who is being deceptive. Does she have your phone number, was she calling you yesterday?" Bridget asked as he looked down at his food and said, "Yes she has my number, and yes she called. But, look at you! You say I am being deceptive. You are trying to tell me nothing happened with Billy?" He asked as he looked hard at her. "No, nothing happened," She griped back. "Really? No touching at all? Because I know how he is," He said pushing her. She stared at the table for a minute. "So, something did happen?" He yelled even louder. "No, he slept by me a few nights and gave me his shirt that is all. He had something going on with a few other girls there, but none of them were me. Oh but, he did give me some peanut butter I had to suck off his fingers," She said making an disgusted face as James looked at her like she had done something unforgivable. She looked back at him feeling somewhat ashamed. "You know what, maybe it is best you leave tonight. I will let the kids sleep here, but you need to leave," He said to her. "What?" She asked surprised, "You are asking me to leave when you are the one who I am sure done so much more. Your mother hinting that you slept with Amy." James shook his head, "I didn't sleep with her you can believe what you want. But, I guarantee I sure didn't suck food off of her body and I didn't have my arms wrapped around her, did he you?" Standing up Bridget started to walk to the door. She knew if James sees her licking that peanut butter off of Billy's hands his mind would wonder. There was no point in arguing with him. "I think it is best we keep the separation agreement in place. It is apparent you don't trust me and I can't trust you so how could we have a marriage? Maybe Amy is best for you," She said as she closed the door gently behind her when she left. James jumped up threw his plate at the sink shattering it. Then he punched the wall and began to cry feeling as though his heart had just been ripped out through his stomach.

CHAPTER 21

When Bridget pulled into the driveway of the empty house she began to cry hysterically. She wondered why she did this to herself again. Why does she keep wanting to give her heart to James when he doesn't really want it? She knew nothing happened with Billy, but James seeing him with his arms around her on the show in September would cause a whole new drama she couldn't deal with. She had to think about her kids. When she was getting out of the car, Billy pulled up behind her. He jumped out of his jeep as she started to walk by the jeep. "What are you doing here?" She said still crying. "Uh, I just wanted to see how you were since we got back from the island," He told her. "I am not really in the mood to chit chat, Billy. Would you please leave?" Standing by his jeep he took a breath for a minute, knowing he should leave. But, he turned around and followed her up to her door. "I thought you would like to go have a drink or something with me? I mean you owe me after all, remember we made a deal on the island? I told you I would give you an idol if you agreed to do something for me in return," He reminded her. She stood still facing her door letting out a loud moaning noise. Throwing her head back and looking up at the sky she said, "I know I promised that, but tonight is not a good night." "No, wrong if you are in a bad mood tonight is the perfect night. To get your mind off of it," He said while standing behind her. While she thought for a moment he took a little smell of her hair without her noticing. "Okay we will go out somewhere, but I don't want to go to that nasty bar you go to," She grumbled throwing her keys in her purse. "Fine with me, Lady," He said excitedly with a huge smile on his face. She turned around to give him a weird look. Bridget jumped into his jeep and looked in the mirror to make sure her makeup wasn't streaming down her face. "I don't really look like we should be going out anywhere," She said wiping the black eyeliner from under her eye. He glanced over at her and said, "You look beautiful without makeup." She laughed and shook her head. "Even with red and puffy eyes?" She asked still giggling. He just smiled and then looked out his window feeling a bit shy. "So, what are you so upset about? I am assuming it has something to do with your jackass husband?" He asked while she shook her head yes. "I don't think we should have ever married. His mother hates me, I am not demure and a beauty. I should have just stayed in Indiana," She said sounding defeated. Billy listened for a minute and said, "Don't do that." She looked over at him fast. "Don't do what?" "Don't do all of the what ifs and how comes, you will drive yourself crazy. I don't live life that way myself. It makes it much easier. Victoria is just the bride of Satan that somehow found her way to our town. She should have stayed in New York. Don't let what she says or does bother you. I think you are great," He said looking over at her. After he finished talking he felt his face blush. He was feeling like an idiot. Bridget stared down at her hands clasped in her lap. "Why do you think I am great? I mean, I am not going to let you in my pants," She said sadly. Billy made a huff sound and looked out his side window. "I think of you as a friend if that is okay? I am just wanting to take you out to have some fun and forget your problems," He said shaking his head frustrated. "But, my problems will still be there when I get back home." She said as she stared out the window. "That is true, but just a few hours of peace of mind is worth it isn't it?" He asked looking over at her. "You don't have to try to be perfect for me. I don't care if you fart or belch what have you, I just want to be your friend," He said as he turned on the jeep radio to break the silence. The song "Broken" By Lifehouse began to play as Bridget was sitting with her head down. All of the sudden Billy heard her start making hysterical sounds. He couldn't tell if she was laughing or crying since her hair was covering her face. He kept looking at her and the road at the same time. "What? I can't tell are you laughing or crying?" He asked a little afraid that he upset her. She raised her head up looking at the ceiling of the jeep laughing so hard that she snorted, "I just….. I just can't believe you told me I could fart." He started to laugh too. "Damn you are so messed up," She said staring out the jeep window. Going through the drive thru of the local Arby's he asked her what she would like to eat. "I don't care, really I am not too hungry," She looked down at her hands. He thought for a minute and said, "I will get us some fries to share would that be okay?" She waved her hand at him, "Sure that is fine." After getting their drinks and fries he drove her to the park. It was dark and they picked a picnic table to sit at near the pond while they ate and talked. Bridget explained the whole situation with James. "So, you know he probably fucked her right?" Billy asked her chomping down on a long twisty fry. She said, "I don't want to think he would do that, but he is a man." She sat for a second and asked, "This is a stupid question I know, but would you do that?" She took in his facial expression when she asked him. She stared long and hard at his face. Chewing up his fry, he took a quick sip of his drink, "This don't go any farther than us, but if I was married….. not ever saying I would be, but if I was married I would like to think I wouldn't cheat." She gave a little chuckle, "You aren't even capable of love so how can you answer that honestly?" He looked at her with a hurtful expression, "Just because I haven't ever been in love before doesn't mean I don't know what it is. I am not this crazy dog that fucks anything it can get its dick in." He started to get a little frustrated by her attitude about the topic. "You know what let's just change the subject," He said throwing the wadded up bag into the trash can by their picnic table. "I am sorry, I didn't mean to upset you," She said. "Not upset. Let's just go, ok?" He said as he began to walk up the grassy hill. She could tell his responses were short with her. They walked down the side walk that led up to the parking lot in the dark. There were lights that lined the side walk so they could see one another's faces. "Can I ask you something?" She said leaning her head far back so she could look up at him since he was so tall. He said, "Sure you can ask me anything I am an open book contrary to popular belief." "Why do you call me lady so much?" He paused for a moment and giggled, "Because you are one. I don't know I just think it suits you." She shook her head no. "What do you mean no?" He asked, "I think you are more of a lady than prom queen Jackie and you are certainly more of a lady than Victoria…. brrrr. I just picture her being all tight and cold when Colton goes to touch her in the bed." Bridget made a gag sound, "Oh gross please I don't want to think of her having sex! You are so weird!" Bridget said laughing. They both just stopped laughing and watched each other's faces as they walked. "Thank you, Billy Hillebrand. You made this night less painful and I appreciate it. I never would have thought you would have such a nice bone in that hard body." She looked down at her feet as she walked. He spoke up staring over at her, "There is a lot of stuff about me you don't know, Lady." Bridget felt a little frustrated saying, "I am not a lady, please stop calling me that." Shoving his hands into his pockets he said, "No, I refuse to stop calling you that. Now can I ask you something?" She giggled and said, "Oh boy, sure go for it." Billy hesitated, "Okay, since I made your night I would appreciate it if you would make my night." She kept staring at him as he stared at his feet walking. "Go on I am waiting?" She said laughing. "Can I kiss you?" He asked. She stopped dead in her tracks as he walked a few steps more. "Kiss me?" She felt her heart start pounding. He had his back to her for a second and then he turned to walk up to her. "I am not asking anything of you, I am just asking for a kiss. I would like to think of this as a date and a kiss would be a perfect ending to it," He said looking away. She thought for a second and then looked right up into his eyes and said, "You know what, I am legally separated and I am sure there is some point during my marriage he has kissed Jackie or Amy so, yeah one kiss shouldn't hurt anything." She wasn't expecting anything extravagant. This was Billy for heaven's sake. He was so rough around the edges. She thought he probably had bad breath seeing as though he never kept his hair trimmed, even though his hair was still an odd turn on to her. She did notice his body smelled very pleasant. He didn't wear strong cologne, but his skin smelled good to her. She thought to herself, he may be able to get many of these other women in the sack easily, but Bridget thought with her mind not just her hormones. She still couldn't help but to feel nervous when he reached out with his left hand and wrapped it around her waist. Not saying a word to her he took her cheek in his right hand slowly moved in to press his lips against hers. He had a goatee and the hair felt silky against her skin. James' goatee felt a little coarse when he would kiss her. Billy kissed her with his lips closed first and then she felt him part his lips. He slid his tongue into her mouth and she felt like her stomach dropped to her feet and her knees felt weak. His breath was so pleasant which shocked her. She reached up and grabbed his neck by his ear, running her finger tips through his fine hair. She pulled his head closer to her so she could press her tongue inside of his mouth. She immediately felt herself get excited and sexually turned on. She melted into the kiss and didn't want to stop. She could feel him become more intense with his kiss. Ashamed, she pulled away and let go of his face. Wiping her mouth off she began to walk off. Billy watched her walk away as he whispered, "wow" under his breath. He ran to catch up to her. "I am sorry if I did something wrong," He said walking at a fast pace to keep up with her. She spoke up fast saying, "No, you didn't I am sorry. I just don't know what I am doing. I am so confused. I am only 24 years old and I am already going to have one failed marriage under my belt. I shouldn't be messing around with you like this." Billy just listened not knowing what to say. He wanted so badly to get to know this woman. He had never felt this way before in his life about a woman. He just wanted a chance with her. Just one chance to see where this feeling would take him. They got into his jeep and he drove her home without saying a word. She leaped out of his jeep with haste and slammed the door shut. She began to walk away, but came back to his car. "Thank you for a nice night, Billy. You aren't as bad as everyone says you are I see that," She didn't know what else to say and she ran to her house not giving him a chance to say anything. The next morning Billy was on cloud 9. He felt amazing. He couldn't hold his enthusiasm any longer he had to tell his brother. He thought it best not to mention anything to Walker. As Billy described his date, Joey noticed a change in his brother. He was floored. It made him happy to see Billy talking this way for a change instead of talking about bedding women. Joey knew better than to tease him. Billy was the type you tease him he clams up and isn't afraid to lash out, even at family. Many a times Billy had beaten up his older brother and cousin. Suddenly, Billy had a serious question he asked Joey, "Do you think I would have a chance with her?" Joey excitedly started to grin. Billy quickly began to talk before Joey had a chance to answer, "I don't mean marriage for god's sake. I mean, you know, just to date. Just me and her, we wouldn't see anyone else." Excitement turned to concern for Joey, "Now hold on little brother she is still married to James Mackenvoy. Are you sure you aren't doing this to get even with him and why the hell did Victoria come to see you the other day?" Billy shook his head, "No, I am not doing this to get even with anyone. I really haven't felt this way before about a woman truly. She is my lady." Joey began to giggle as Billy went on, "And Victoria, she is just a trouble making hussy. She wants Bridget out of her family." Joey sternly asked, "So she is recruiting you? Won't that put a kink in your relationship with Bridget?" Billy replied quickly, "No, because I am not doing this for that bitch or James. I am doing this for me and Bridget. I always go for whatever I want and I want her. I know I can make her happy. James is a fucking fool. If he is dumb enough to let her go I will gladly take her. If he wants to go date those stuck up rich broads that have enough plastic in their faces to make Halloween masks, let him. I would like to date Bridget. I am 25 years old and I haven't even had someone I would feel comfortable calling a girlfriend until now," Billy finished talking for a minute. "Alright little brother, if you want this all of your family will be behind you," Joey said as Billy spoke up, "Don't tell any of the family only you know this. I don't want anyone knowing this. I am not in love with the girl, I just want to date her to see how I feel. So keep it quiet for me." Joey agreed. James' day wasn't starting off so good. He was miserable. He wanted his wife and he didn't know what to do or what to say to get her back. How could he battle with his mother? She would always win, no matter what he would do, she would win. But, he had to try. Dialing Bridget's cell phone number his heart started to speed up. When she answered he asked her to come over to see the kids. It was selfish on his part. He wanted to see her badly and he knew she wouldn't stay away from those kids. He rushed upstairs to clean up his goatee and spray on cologne when she was on her way over. When she showed up she noticed how nice he looked and she started feeling those urgings again. "Hello James," She said to him. "Hi," He said walking over to kiss her on the cheek. "Momma!" Megan yelled running up to her. Dylan's little legs were running as fast as they could carry him. She was so happy to see her kids. "I thought maybe we could all do something fun today, maybe go to the park," James said when she raised up in a shocked manner. "The park? Why?" She asked in a wild voice. James noticed her jumpiness. She thought it was his way of saying he knew she was with Billy the night before. "Yes, the park that is where kids play," He sarcastically said. Bridget stood for a moment stoic. Bridget thought about Victoria snooping and felt great guilt about the night before. "James, I don't want to keep secrets from you. When we were on the island Billy did keep me warm during some of the nights it was cold. And last night he took me out for French fries and gave me a kiss," She could see the pain and hurt on James' face. He turned his back to her as he tried to compose himself. "Billy Hillenbrand. Why would you do this to me?" He asked her rubbing his forehead roughly. "I didn't do anything bad, James. The island thing was nothing and that last night…. I am so confused. I just don't know what I am supposed to do. I want to be with you so bad, but your mom won't stop interfering." He turned back around to look at her, "So are you wanting to be with him now is that it?" She glanced down at the kids and back at James. "No, I want to be with you. I won't lie, Billy is attractive, but I am sure you feel the same way about Jackie and Amy so please cut me some slack there," She said with tears in her eyes. He reached out grabbing her and pulling her close to him. He kissed her very hard and passionately. When he stopped kissing her he looked into her eyes deeply, "I don't want to lose you, do you hear me? Am I making sense to you? I don't want to lose you. I am sorry I wasn't a good husband to you. I am trying here. I am going to make mistakes. But, from now on I will try my best to trust you." She interrupted him, "Yeah I know, where have I heard that before?" "It will be different this time baby I swear. Just give me a chance," He said. She felt tears stinging her eyes, "I want to so bad, I don't want our marriage to end… but your momma, James, I can't take it. Why can't we just move away from this town? Please, why can't we just load up the kids and our stuff and move to whatever other state you want to I just have to get away from your mother." He thought, trying to find the right words to say. "You are asking me to leave my whole family behind. My daddy wouldn't get to see my babies. I wouldn't get to see my brother or cousin, how could I do that?" She was so angry with him. After all, she did just that same thing to move down to Tennessee to be with him. She left her family behind. She couldn't help to feel like James was so selfish. What would she do? Should she give him another chance? She knew there was no point in hanging around with Billy. She didn't love him anyway, she just enjoyed his company and he was a wonderful kisser. James she loved completely, she had so many years with him already. But, she just felt as though James didn't love her the same way. True he may fight for her, but to her that wasn't the way to show her his love. If he could cut his mother out of his life forever, that would be a testament of his love for her. But, she knew that was a lot to ask of him, of anyone.

CHAPTER 22

It was a beautiful hot August day. Bridget enjoyed spending the day with James and her kids. It felt nice. All of the difficult times were pushed away from her mind for those few hours. They felt like a family again. The next two days Bridget never went back to her rental house, she stayed with James. She didn't feel comfortable making love to James at that time so she didn't. She wanted to figure out what was going on in her mind and heart. Every time she would make love to him she would become confused. She would forget all about his selfishness, the secrets and of course his mother. Cullen and Marcus wanted to see James' marriage work out. They knew Bridget was a fantastic lady and he was lucky to have her no matter what Victoria thought. Everyone in the family adored her. She was a fantastic cook. Victoria had a personal chef who made food for the family and catered to their picnics, but Bridget made all of her food from scratch. Around Christmas all of the men of the family fought over her famous dips and cheese spreads she would make. Bridget was the type of woman who was pure and real. Even Colton and Rick knew this. They had always treated her well, except for the few times they would have to reign her in for her mouth. Cullen and Giselle never married. Motherhood didn't suit her as well as it did the other girls. She moved back to Brazil and Cullen kept full custody of Caleb, his pride and joy. Caleb would still spend quality time throughout the year with his momma. After the weekend Bridget mentioned to James she thought it would be best if they take things slowly. Which meant she wanted to stay at her rental house during the week and they would both spend every day with the kids. Her kids were the most important thing on her mind. She wanted to do things right. She felt that if she stayed at her rental while she and James tried to figure out their marriage, maybe Victoria would leave them alone thinking it was over. Bridget's whole plan was to eventually talk James into leaving town. She felt sooner or later she could convince him that it was the right thing to do. She was sadly mistaken. Her first night back at her rental Billy showed up to visit. The kids would always stay the night at James' house so they wouldn't feel out of sorts during the separation. On this night they would stay all night with Victoria. When Billy showed up at Bridget's house she answered the door reluctantly. When she opened the door he smiled happily at her and said, "Hey, how are you? I haven't spoken to you for a few days." She kept looking down instead of into his eyes. "Yeah, James and I have decided to make this marriage work. We are going to try." Billy just looked at her as she finally glanced up into his eyes. "Why would you do this? You know he is just going to hurt you again," Billy said obviously feeling hurt. Bridget quickly said to him, "No, not this time. I am going to make sure we do things differently. It was all Victoria's fault before." Billy shook his head saying, "No if he truly loved you he wouldn't let her hurt you. I thought you were smarter than this." Billy began stomping off as Bridget yelled behind him, "Once again how the hell do you know what love is? You have no right to say that to me!" She slammed the door shut as he sped away angrily. She was terribly upset and reached for her phone to call James. Billy sped off heading to his usual hangout, the bar to drink with Rodney. He wanted to drown out his feelings of jealousy and anger. Why should he care anyway he thought to himself? James answered his phone happy to hear Bridget's voice on the other end. She didn't tell him about Billy showing up, she just wanted to hear James' voice. After hanging up the phone James heard a knock at the door. It was Jackie. She visited with him for a few hours just talking about usual things when it turned personal. "So, you and Bridget are still separated?" She asked grabbing his knee and rubbing it as they sat on the sofa. He explained to her about the kiss between Bridget and Billy. "She doesn't deserve you. I know that and your momma knows that. Why can't you see that?" Jackie asked him in her raspy voice. He looked into her face and she leaned forward deeply kissing him. He didn't push her away right away. After all, didn't Bridget do the same thing? He felt as though he was getting even. Jackie rubbed his thigh and worked her way up to his crotch. Massaging his package she could feel him start to get an erection. She grabbed a hold of his crotch as they kissed passionately. Suddenly, he pushed her away and said, "Woe, wait a minute. We can't do this." "Why not? You are separated you can do what you want," She said as she again started to kiss him and he kissed her back for a moment. "No, I can't if I am wanting my wife back," He said pushing her away. Really upset Jackie jumped up off the couch. "How can you be so blind, James? I love you and I would never treat you the way she is treating you!" Jackie yelled. "It isn't just her, she and I have both done things to mess up and I am not the best husband in the world here. Maybe one day momma will see Bridget and I love each other deeply and she will accept it," He said in a sullen voice. Jackie angrily grabbed her purse and rushed out the door. Billy was sloppy drunk as he stumbled out of the bar walking up to his jeep. Knowing he shouldn't be driving he still shoved the key in the hole and swerved over to Bridget's house. Falling out of his jeep he rushed up to her door pounding crazily. She opened the door surprised to see him back. "What the hell?" She yelled. "You know what? You are a stubborn annoying girl. And, I don't know why any man would put up with your shit!" He stuttered as she looked at him confused. "You are drunk, come in here. You are not getting in that car. You will end up killing yourself or worse yet someone else." She said pulling on his shirt. He fell on his face as he came in the door and he began to laugh hysterically at himself. "Look, I am going to put you in the spare bedroom and tomorrow morning you have to get the hell out of here got it?" She grumbled. He didn't answer as she helped him to the bedroom. As he pulled off his shirt she stared for a moment at his hard chiseled chest. His chest didn't have any hair on it, but his belly button all the way down to his crotch was covered with dark blonde hair. After daydreaming at his body for a moment she snapped out of it and sat a trash can down beside his bed. "There is the bathroom if you have to piss and here is a trashcan if you have to puke. I would appreciate it if you don't ruin my bed or floor." She said walking out of the room and turning off the light. He shook his head yes as he began to pass out. She watched him for a while before heading to her room for the night. Jackie headed over to Bridget's house to speak with her about James. She already had her speech prepared in her head to get her to leave James for good. When she pulled up she seen Billy's jeep parked halfway in the yard and halfway in the driveway. With her mouth gaping open she phoned Victoria and told her. "NO, don't go to the door. Take a few photos on your cell phone of his jeep sitting there," Victoria demanded to Jackie. She did as she was told. She figured she would wait until the next morning to talk to Bridget and she would use that photo as blackmail. She giggled with delight as she pulled away from Bridget's house. Victoria calmly hung up her phone smiling. Colton never knew about any of Victoria's antics. He was too involved in his business to care. But, if he knew how responsible she was for a lot of the things that had happened over the past several years, he would have been appalled. That is not the way Mackenvoys behave in his mind. They are ruthless and fight head on, they don't play petty games. Besides he liked Bridget. He didn't like the fact Emma became pregnant by a Hillenbrand, but he would not have condoned any type of deception whereas the miscarriage was concerned. But, things were looking great for Emma. She was happily married and had a daughter named Roxy. Victoria believed everything she did would end with superb results. The next morning, very early, Jackie headed over to Bridget's to talk to her before work. She was stunned to see Billy's jeep still in the driveway. She was absolutely shocked. Could Bridget really have had a fling with Billy? She rushed back over to James' house without calling Victoria yet. She wanted to see how things would play out first. Once she rushed into James' house Jackie told him what she saw the night before and where she just came from. He looked at her in disbelief. "She wouldn't do that to me, Jackie. She wouldn't," James said with a shaky voice. She reached down into her purse and pulled out her cell phone. She held up the photo on her phone of his jeep right by her house. He started to feel sick and enraged. "Take me there," He said rushing out to her car. She happily obliged with a smile on her face. She sped as fast as she could so Billy wouldn't have time to leave. When they pulled up, Billy was still there. They both hopped out of the car and James rushed up to the door twisting the knob and beating on the door. Bridget had already given Billy his coffee to get him woke up as she started to walk slowly to the door. She heard James yelling and tried to think in her mind what she could say. She knew how this looked. He started to walk off the porch when Bridget opened the door gently. Still trying to figure out how she could explain why she was in her night shirt and panties with Billy Hillenbrand inside. She began to speak while James stood at the bottom of the porch steps staring at her. "This isn't what it looks like," She said holding up her hands. Jackie shouted, "Oh yeah right it never is, is it?" Bridget became angry and yelled, "Mind your own business psycho skank!" Bridget shouted back. James just continued to stare at her with pain in his eyes, not saying a word. Billy came strolling halfway out the front door with no shirt on and said, "What the fuck is going on our here?" Bridget started to turn around to talk to him, but before she had a chance James lunged up onto the porch and slammed into Billy breaking the front door as they flew onto the floor. James brutally wailed his fist against Billy's face. Billy wasn't ready for this type of fight so he took most of the adrenaline James was beating into his face and sides. Bridget and Jackie came running in trying to stop the fight. James raised up as he started to punch Billy hard in the head and accidentally knocked Bridget off her feet, sending her slamming into the table by the television. Jackie begged James to stop and asked him to go. After he was done hitting Billy, he stood up and looked at Bridget. "You are not my wife, you are a fucking whore. I don't know who you are. My momma was right about you," James said extremely loudly. Bridget felt crushed and began to cry. Billy was making grumbling noises as he started to sit up. James and Jackie went walking out of the house and as they headed to the car Bridget ran to the front door screaming. "James, James please god, I didn't do anything! I swear to you I love you! I didn't do anything!" She continued to scream as they pulled off in Jackie's car. Jackie flashed Bridget a quick smile to let her know she won. Billy stood up after being beaten so badly and wiped the blood off of his mouth and nose. "You know I only lost that one because I am hung over," He said as she ignored what he said. Bridget cried as she stared out the front door at nothing, then she turned around and looked at Billy. He stood there staring at her, using his shirt he picked up off the floor to clean the blood off his face. "He called me a whore and he said I am what his mother says I am," Bridget said stunned with tears pouring down her cheeks. "Yeah, well I told you he is an asshole. He didn't even know what happened here he just assumed," Billy said in a nonchalant manner. After standing for a moment and letting it sink in what he had just said to her she started to get angry. How dare he show up with Jackie and treat her this way? She stared at Billy's cleanly wiped face and suddenly rushed over into his arms and began kissing him. He felt shocked and grabbed her face to look at her for a moment. "I want you to make love to me," She said as he was still holding her face in his hands.

"Just do it and make it go away," She begged as she started pulling at his jeans he was wearing. The whole time he was confused as to what was going on, but he couldn't stop himself. Reaching under her night shirt he grabbed a hold of her panties and ripped them off, tearing them in the process. He picked her up and flopped her down onto the couch and continued to passionately kiss her. Rubbing her fingers through his long fine hair she then grabbed a hold of his erection. "Please just wet it and put it inside of me. Hurry!" She pushed with her words breathing heavily. She didn't want to have time to think or else she would change her mind. She had to hurt James as much as he hurt her with his words. He licked his fingers and gently stuck them inside her so he could get her ready for him. He grabbed his hard on not bothering to stop and use a condom. He pushed himself inside of her. She gasped as she flung her head back, "Yes, please don't stop, Billy, just don't stop!" She yelled. He began pumping harder as he buried his face in her breast and held onto her body. He wasn't as big as James was, but he wasn't a small man either. He pushed into her and she could feel herself get wetter and more excited with each pump of his hips. Getting ready to come he pulled himself out of her as they both gasped for breath. He laid his head on her breasts for a moment breathing heavily. As she realized what she had just done, she asked him to leave. "Please, Billy, just go," She said as she turned on her side and began to cry. He raised up and stared at her, feeling a little sick. He didn't want her to regret what had just happened. He didn't regret it, but he didn't picture it being that way either. He buttoned up his pants and grabbed his shirt. He didn't say a word to her as he left the house. James immediately called Victoria right away to tell her what had happened and that he wouldn't be at work that day. He felt completely crushed. He was so sick to his stomach he had to ask Jackie to pull over. He jumped out of the car and began throwing up. Jackie sat with her elbow resting on the car door. She felt at peace while he wretched by the side of the road. He slowly got back into the car crying. "How could she do this to me? How could she fucking do this?" He asked Jackie. "I don't know, James. But, it will be okay. We will all be here for you." Victoria immediately called Marcus and told him what happened so he could get the divorce papers started. He was shocked. He couldn't believe Bridget would do something like that. Neither did Olivia, Cindy or Cullen. Before they passed judgment, Cullen and Olivia thought it would be best if they go see Bridget to find out exactly what happened that night.

CHAPTER 23

When Olivia and Cullen arrived at Bridget's house, she was sitting outside on the porch looking lost. Olivia ran up to her and asked, "Honey, are you ok? What happened?" Bridget sat for a moment staring off into space. "Why does it matter? You won't believe a word I say," She said sullenly as Cullen stepped in front of her. Olivia rubbed her back and reassured her, "That's not true. We aren't judgmental at all just tell us what happened." Bridget explained what all happened the night before to them. When she got to the part where James and Billy fought she began to cry uncontrollably. Olivia looked at her confused. Bridget started sobbing louder as she said, "He told me I was a whore, oh god he told me I was a whore like Victoria says." Olivia looked up at Cullen with a shocked face. Cullen spoke up and said, "Wait, he didn't even ask you what happened he just assumed you had sex with Billy?" Bridget shook her head yes. "Well, that isn't right. He shouldn't have done that. I am going to go talk to him and let him know he was mistaken." Cullen said starting to walk away when Bridget stopped him by shouting. "NO wait! Please, Cullen don't. It is over, my marriage is over. It is for certain now," Bridget said while Olivia shook her head. "No, no honey. James gets a little hot headed sometimes and doesn't think when he is emotional you know that. Victoria is bad about messing with his head," Olivia said as she tried to make her feel better. Bridget kept shaking her head, "No it is over. He hates me." Cullen stood looking at her as she cried. "So you are going to just give up? Fight her for god's sake. Don't let her do this to you. I adore uncle Colton, but Victoria is definitely an evil old bitch. You need to fight for your kids," Cullen said feeling frustrated with her. Bridget jumped up, "Just stop! It is over! I don't want anything from him except child support. I don't want his money no matter what Victoria thinks. I just want to divorce and let him get on with his life." Olivia stared at the ground extremely upset. She knew James and Bridget belonged together. "I think if you two just sit down and talk about this it will all work itself out," Olivia said trying to talk her down. Bridget angrily turned around and said, "Yeah well, that is easy for you to say. She don't hate you like she does me. She don't interfere in your marriage like she does mine. James looked at me like she looks at me." Bridget just stared at Olivia. "So, I did exactly what he thought I did," Bridget said looking at her fingers as she picked at her nails. "What?!" Cullen shouted walking up to her. "I did what I wanted to do. This is what he wanted all along. He wanted a way out and he thought he would use me to get it. So I slept with Billy," Bridget said stone faced looking back and forth at them both. "And I don't feel guilty about it," She finished as she walked up the steps to go into her house. Olivia and Cullen didn't know what to say. They just stared at each other stunned. "Oh my god, Cobra. It is really over between them isn't it?" Olivia began to get tears in her eyes. "I think, she is hurt and confused. I think she done something she ordinarily wouldn't have done without being pushed so far. Come on Olivia let's get out of here," Cullen said. They both got into the car and left her house. Back at James' house he sat motionless staring at a blank screen on the television. Jackie came walking up to him and breathed the words, "James. Don't let this ruin you." He looked up at her and hopped up fast heading to the kitchen. She followed him as he rushed down the hallway. "What are you doing?" She asked him while he rummaged around the refrigerator for his whiskey. Pulling out the bottle he took four huge shots as Jackie begged him not to get drunk. "Come on she isn't worth it. Stop it!" She shouted as she yanked the bottle out of his hand and sat it on the counter. He reached over, grabbed her and started kissing her very hard. She began to breathe heavily as he ripped her shirt off. He slammed her down on the kitchen table and as she laid on her back he pulled her panties off from under her skirt. Very fast, he unbuttoned his pants and shoved himself into her, pressing his weight on her thighs. She could easily handle the size of him. She moaned in pleasure as she whispered his name into his ear, "Yes James, make love to me." He listened to her repeat it over and over. He came very quickly. Jumping back and zipping his pants back up, he stared at her breathing heavily. She raised up on her elbows staring back at him. "Are you okay?" She asked him. Just then the front door opened. Cullen and Olivia came walking down the hallway very fast to see both James and Jackie looking guilty. Jackie immediately jumped off the table and fixed her top. "Oh my god you have to be fucking kidding me!" Olivia shouted disgusted. Cullen shook his head and shouted at him, "Who the hell are you?" James looked at him for a second and said, "What do you mean who the hell am I? I am someone whose wife ripped his fucking heart out and spit on it right in front of him that is who I am!" Cullen began to shake his head and laugh. "You have it all wrong, man. Little miss bombshell there and your mother have got you all backwards and the only person at fault for losing your wife is you. You two just keep fucking up a storm don't let Olivia or I stop you," Cullen said disgusted as he headed on down the hallway to leave. Olivia looked to Jackie, "Why? They have kids together how can you do this shit?" Jackie looked at her surprised and asked, "Me? I think you need to be blaming his wife." Cullen came walking back down the hallway and said, "No it is you and Victoria! You both orchestrated this and it worked like a charm didn't it?" He shouted at Jackie. Jackie shook her head and said, "I don't know what the fuck you are talking about." Cullen became even more frustrated and said, "Yes you do know what I am talking about! James, Bridget didn't fuck Billy last night. In fact, had you stayed around to talk to her you would have found out that he was sleeping in a whole other room. There was no sex, she was just trying to keep him from hurting someone else. The asshole was driving drunk. But, Jackie just used what she seen and spun it into a big huge lie, didn't you?" He looked directly at her as James stood day dreaming at the table. "My wife didn't sleep with him? OH my god, and I just…" Before he could finish the sentence Cullen interrupted, "Wrong. You lost the best thing that ever happened to you. And what is sad, it's those nasty words that came out of your mouth. You called her a whore and made her feel like she was trash. Just like your mommy dearest. So yes, she did go ahead and fuck him." James shook his head confused and yelled, "What, wait?" Cullen went on to say, "If you would have stuck around and talked to her you would have known nothing happened. But, hey no matter you are here fucking Jackie anyway, right? I am getting the hell out of here, the stench in this room makes me want to puke!" Cullen turned to leave the house sickened by the whole situation. Olivia just shook her head and said, "I am so ashamed of you, James." She turned and walked out of the house leaving Jackie and James alone. James stared at the floor in disgust and whispered, "What have I done?" Jackie came walking up to him, but he put his hand up. "Please, leave my house," James whispered. Jackie didn't say a word as she left the house. Bridget took her clothes off and stood in the shower. She began to cry and thought what a mess of her life she has made. She wasn't thinking so much about what she did with Billy, she was thinking about what James had said to her. She could still hear his words calling her a whore over and over in her mind. When she stepped out of the shower she could hear something in the living room. Throwing on her clothes she came out to find Billy fixing the front door that was busted in just a few hours earlier. She walked up to him slowly. He turned around and seen her. He looked back at the door he was working on and said, "Hey I figured I would fix this for you. No reason to leave it like that. It wouldn't be safe." He continued to work as she sat down at the small kitchen table off to right of him. She sat quiet for a minute and then started to talk. "Please, forget what happened between us earlier. I mean, I am sure you got what you wanted," She said watching him work. Sitting down his screw driver he turned to face her. "Got what I wanted? You still think that way of me, huh? I mean as I recall you were the one all over me," He told her while she looked down at the table. "Yes, but I wouldn't have done that if James hadn't said what he did. I just want you to know that I don't just sleep with people. So if you are hoping for another romp it isn't going to happen," She said staring at him out of the corner of her eye. He worked on the door until he finished. He grabbed his bag of tools off the floor and he said to her, "I don't expect anything from you, don't worry about it. I hope everything works out for you the way you hope it will." He left her sitting there still stewing over the fact that her marriage was over. Billy never told anyone except Joey about sleeping with Bridget. Joey kept it to himself as Billy requested. She wasn't a conquest to him. Bridget had Olivia pick up her kids from Victoria, she couldn't stand to look at her. James and Bridget didn't speak for the next two weeks. Olivia did all of the exchanging of the kids. Marcus never drew up any papers until James was ready. Olivia told Bridget about James and Jackie. She was very sickened by it, but figured that is what he deserved anyway. After two weeks of not talking to one another, James showed up at Bridget's house. She hadn't spoken to Billy either, since the day he fixed her door. When she opened her door to see James she assumed it was about the papers. "Yes, what can I do for you?" She asked him. "May I come in?" He asked quietly. "Where is the kids? Are they in the car?" She asked looking off at his mustang sitting in the driveway. "No, I asked momma to keep them for a while," He said while Bridget opened the door to let him in. "I am guessing you are wanting to talk about the divorce?" She asked him as he sat down at the kitchen table. "I want to talk about our communication. We are not on the same page, ever it seems like. I know we both lost somehow over the years the trust, but we never lost the love for each other. I know I made mistakes, and you aren't an angel either," He stopped talking for a minute to look at her. "I know I am not an angel in all this, James. I did what I did. I am not blaming you for that, I am taking full responsibility for that. I made the choice to do it, no matter what you said to me. I am sorry for hurting you," She started to cry. "I am sorry for hurting you, Bridget. I have been stupid and hot headed for almost all of our marriage. I know we are separated, but I have to tell you knowing you slept with that sick son of a bitch feels like you cheated on our marriage," He explained as she started to fidget. "Well now you know how I felt every time I wondered if you slept with Amy or Jackie. And I know you slept with Jackie the same day I slept with Billy," She said hatefully. He thought for a few seconds and then asked, "So what was it revenge?" "Honestly, yes I felt like I was getting even with you for hurting me all these years. I am sorry I was in a bad state of mind at the time. If I could have done things differently, I would have," She explained. He shook his head and agreed he would have as well. "You live and you learn, right? But, I can't let you go still. Can you tell me why?" He asked looking deep into her eyes. She was surprised when he asked this. "You still want us to save this marriage?" She asked shocked. "I love you, we both made mistakes. I want to start over. But, don't think for a second this is over between me and Hillenbrand because it isn't. If you can let me have my vengeance against him, just this once, then I can forgive what you did. But I will never forget," He said staring at her as he waited for her answer. "So let me get this straight, you are asking me to be okay with you going after Billy again and you will forgive me? What about me? I mean you slept with Jackie, too. Where the hell is my vengeance?" She asked angrily. He listened to her and said, "I will kindly fire her as my assistant and I will tell momma to butt out of our marriage. I will tell momma if she don't leave you alone, she will lose me. Plain and simple. I will do that right as I leave this house, if you promise me you will try too? You need to stay away from Billy because I can't take it, do you understand that? I can't take it." Bridget nodded in agreement. He leaned over and kissed her gently on her lips. "We will take this slow, and I will stop making you feel second best. But, please don't talk to that shit Hillenbrand. He is not a friend to you," He said. Bridget sat in silence and then said, "I know, I know Billy just wanted in my pants I am not an idiot James. Well, I kind of am when it comes to you. I haven't spoken to Billy for weeks. You would really get rid of Jackie and put your momma in her place?" He shook his head yes smiling, "I have already even told Amy I am not interested in her, she is on a plane back to New York." Bridget began to cry. "I mean what I say, Bridget, I am done with momma interfering. Cullen helped me see it. If she don't stop we will move out of this town and never look back," He said and Bridget felt like finally she was getting what she wanted. Bridget heard the words she had longed to hear for five years.

CHAPTER 24

After leaving Bridget's house, James headed straight to his mother's house to speak with her. He was very nervous. She was a force to be reckoned with and he knew it. But, he was serious about wanting to save his marriage. Although, he was so disgusted and hurt by what Bridget had done, he knew he was at fault too. At first, Victoria was delighted to see her son. She walked up with joy and kissed him on the cheek. She thought she was about to get some wonderful news about his impending divorce. "Momma, I am not going to mince words here. I am done, okay. I can't take your disrespect to my wife any longer. I love her, we are going to fight to save this marriage. My kids need us to be the best parents we can be and we can't do that when you are constantly throwing women at me," He said with a tremble in his voice. Victoria stared at him with a nasty evil look. "She is a whore and she cheated on you…" Victoria said as James raised his voice interrupting her, "Oh momma stop it! She isn't a whore. Anything that has happened is because of me and worst yet because of you!" Victoria walked up to him smacking him hard across the face and she shouted, "Don't you talk to me in that manner! She was intimate with that dog from the hills and you want to tell me she isn't a whore?" James was staring off to the side then his eyes moved to hers. "You lay off my wife, you lay off of me or so help me Christ, you will lose me and you will lose your grandchildren. Do you got it?" He asked her hatefully. Victoria stood stone cold as James turned to walk out of the room. When he reached his car he took a deep breath. He could feel the chill in the room as he left his mother. The next stop was his father's office. He walked in full of anxiety. He was afraid of his momma, but his daddy terrified him. Colton was in a meeting when he strolled into his office. "Well hey there son, let's wrap this up so I can talk to my boy for a bit," Colton said as everyone stood up to leave the office. "So, son, how are you holding up? I heard about the silly shit with Bridget. I never would have thought she would do that," Colton said leaning back in his chair. James told Colton he was mistaken and explained the situation. After he was done explaining he gave Colton the bad news. "Daddy, it is momma. She put all these events in motion to make me doubt my wife. She tried to make Bridget doubt me," James said as Colton made a pinched face. "Now son, you can't blame your momma for what happened in your marriage," Colton tried to reason with him, but James shook his head and said, "Yes I can daddy. I am done, I am tired. It is time for me to step up and start being a man. I am not a momma's boy, but yet I get teased hard core about that. I just want you to know I am going to come in to work like I am supposed to, I am going to be the best husband and father I can be and most of all I am going to be a tougher son for you. I am cutting the apron strings momma tries to keep me with." Colton smiled as he heard his son speak. He couldn't help to feel very proud of James in that moment. "Congratulations my boy, now you know what it is like to be a man," Colton said as he smiled from ear to ear. James smiled staring down and said, "Don't get too excited yet daddy, I also want you to fire Jackie. She can't be my assistant and I really don't want her working here. It would help out my marriage a lot if I don't have to see her daily. I have done something stupid as you know…" Colton interrupted James and said, "Don't worry about it son, we will give her the option to resign so it won't sting as much. You work on that marriage." James stood up and nodded at Colton. As he left his father's office he felt very relieved. His father sure surprised him. James felt like a man and he felt accepted for the first time in his life. All he ever wanted was to make his father proud, his mother not so much. And all he had ever wanted was Bridget in his life as his wife. Things felt like they were looking up. His last stop was Jackie. He went into his office to see her sitting at his desk. "Hey, stranger I wasn't sure if you were coming in today," She said while he shut the door quietly behind him. "I am taking work home with me today," He said as he sat down. She stared at him in a curious way. He leaned forward and started to explain, "Listen, I know this may seem extreme and hurtful to you. And I don't want to seem insensitive to you since I know you have feelings for me. But, we can't continue working together. Especially, after what happened between us. I know we have a long history together, but I am sorry to say I don't feel like I can trust you." Jackie became upset and raised her voice as she shouted, "She is putting you up to this isn't she? You are actually staying with her?" James shook his head and looked out the window. Jackie couldn't believe what she was hearing. "Jackie, she and I have made mistakes, we are in love and we want to make things work. I was an idiot for a lot of years and that ends today. I almost threw away the best thing that ever happened to me and I have gotten wise. Maybe someday we can be friends again, but right now it isn't an option. I am sorry, but you have got to let go. You take care now," He said as he stood up and walked out of the office. Jackie became enraged and pushed his books off of his desk. She couldn't let Bridget get away with this. James decided he wouldn't watch the show Bridget and Billy were on in September, he thought it best to keep things calm with his wife. The next two months James and Bridget became very close again. It was like they were getting a second chance at their marriage. Bridget and James couldn't have been happier. The Halloween party was a blast that year. Bridget would see Billy from time to time around town, but she would never say anything. At the Halloween party Bridget stayed close to James' side. She never wanted to give Billy the opportunity to mess up her marriage. She promised James and she would stick to that promise. Victoria left Bridget alone for the time being. She didn't want to lose her son, but that didn't mean she had given up. Not by a long shot in fact. At the end of October Bridget noticed she had missed her period, although she did have a short one at the end of September. She had been irregular before so she wasn't too concerned. But, the second week of November she began feeling sick and started vomiting all day. She didn't want to say anything to James unless she was sure. She bought a pregnancy test and to her surprise it was positive! She couldn't wait to tell Cindy and Olivia. James was ecstatic! He wanted to have at least six babies with her. James and Bridget didn't plan on telling Victoria or Colton until Christmas as a surprise, but the baby had other plans. During the annual family Thanksgiving dinner while everyone was sitting around the table about ready to dive into their huge helpings of turkey and mashed potatoes, Bridget began feeling sick. She was hoping the feeling would pass as it would tend to do at times. But, she knew it was a bit too late as she rushed up from her seat holding the vomit in her mouth. She managed to make it to the trash can sitting in the dining room. As Bridget wretched everyone looked at their plates of food suddenly losing their appetites. "If she was sick she should not have come here," Victoria said with a disgusted tone. James giggled and said, "She isn't sick, she is pregnant." Emma screamed in delight. She was very happy for them. After having Roxy, she wasn't able to have any more babies due to complications so knowing her brother was having more made her very happy. Colton and Rick congratulated James although Olivia, Marcus and Cullen already knew. Coming back to the table Bridget apologized profusely. "Nonsense darling, you can't help it if you are sick," Colton said kindly. At the beginning of December not only did Bridget find out she won first place on the show and the million dollars, but she also had her first ultrasound. She and James were so excited. During the test all the sudden the technician said, "Uh oh, I hope you two are ready to have your hands full." Bridget raised her head up frightened and asked, "Why, what is wrong?" The nurse tried to reassure her, "Oh don't be alarmed, you are having twins so congratulations." Bridget and James looked at one another excited. He gave her several kisses as he smiled with excitement. After the ultrasound the doctor came into the room to talk to them. "Ok so I see you are having twins, congratulations. Now, I also see Bridget that you had a period in September is that right?" He looked at her a little concerned. "Yes, it was very light, but it lasted for about four days," She said noticing his puzzled face. The doctor shook his head and said, "Well, my dear going by the growth of the twins you are actually due in May not June. You are a whole month ahead." Bridget stared at him surprised while James felt his stomach flip up into his throat. "Wait a minute I had a period though," Bridget said feeling scared. The doctor began to explain in a cheerful manner, "Yes, sometimes women can have a light period at the beginning of a pregnancy. I have even seen some have a period up to the fourth month. It is nothing to be too concerned about. You are just a little farther along than we thought. Looks like the last week of August is when you became pregnant." Bridget began to cry while James rubbed his face saying, "Please god no." The doctor was confused until Bridget explained what had happened in the exact week he was talking about. "I see, well to make you feel better we can do an amnio in January or February to see who the lucky guy is," The doctor said trying to joke a little bit. James and Bridget were not in a joking mood. They both left the doctor's office not knowing what to say. Joey's wife heard about the doctor's appointment from someone who knew Olivia. Billy didn't hear anything about it. He was working on a house when Joey ran to find him. "Billy! Hey Billy!" Joey yelled as he ran up to him laughing. "What you dip shit I am right here," Billy said in a grumpy mood. Joey smacked him on the back and said breathlessly, "Hey, you ugly shit! Did you know about Bridget?" Banging nails into the wood Billy turned his head around to talk to him. "If I wanted to know anything about her or that asshole of a husband of hers I would ask. I don't want to know," Billy grumbled. Joey laughed as he said, "Oh you want to know this my brother." Billy stared at him eagerly waiting for this wonderful news he was so excited to tell. "You may be a father soon," Joey said holding out his arms. Billy shook his head and said, "Man don't even fucking joke about something like that." Joey couldn't stop laughing even though he was still out of breath. "I am serious Billy, she is pregnant and they found out it happened at the end of August. Do you know what that means you oaf?" Joey asked when Billy turned around fast in a state of shock and said, "No fucking way, are you fucking kidding me?" "NO, I am not kidding you. But, I am surprised you didn't wear a rubber," Joey said sarcastically. "At the moment I wasn't thinking of covering it all I could think about was seeing what she felt like," Billy said daydreaming at the ground. Joey just laughed shaking his head and said, "One time my brother that is all it takes, one time. We may be having kids the same age isn't that amazing?!" Billy looked down half smiling and said, "I am sure it isn't mine though." As Joey started to walk off he mumbled, "By the way, it isn't one baby it is two. As in twins." Billy quickly turned around to watch Joey walk away and whispered, "Twins? Oh my god."

CHAPTER 25

James was so happy for the past few months. He had put it out of his mind about getting even with Billy for sleeping with his wife. But, this news was tearing him apart. Bridget was just as torn up. She couldn't understand why she was being punished. What did she do to deserve this? Finally, James had seen what he was doing wrong. He had thrown his selfishness away, but for what? For this? Bridget felt extremely ashamed since this was all on her. She may have thought James' harsh words lead up to what had happened, but she knew that this one was on her. James was still being very good to her. He didn't treat her with disgust or even malice. James was accepting his part of the responsibility. Had he grown up sooner, this wouldn't be happening. The news reached Colton, Rick and worse Victoria. At Christmas, everyone treated Bridget as if nothing was wrong. Of course, Victoria couldn't help but give her nasty glances. Strangely, she didn't say a word about the babies or threaten her in any way. Bridget couldn't help but wonder what she was up to. Victoria definitely hoped that this would work out in her favor. Just maybe that idiot Billy Hillenbrand did his job too well, Victoria thought. She figured she shouldn't have to interfere if Bridget was, in fact, carrying Billy's twins. The New Year's Eve dance was as beautiful as it always was. Bridget's belly was now showing under her cute little dress. With twins, she was showing quicker than normal. None of the Hillenbrand clan acknowledged her. Billy certainly couldn't stop staring at her. Every time James would glance over his way, Billy would turn his head as if he wasn't interested. Billy had even brought a date to the dance which was different for him. He never brought dates to their dances. Bridget felt as though he was making a statement to her that he wasn't interested in being a father. Or maybe he was just showing her he knew he wasn't possibly the father of the twins. She prayed every night those babies belonged to James. That night, when the New Year rung in that was her only wish. She closed her eyes, while everyone else counted down, she just prayed hoping god would hear her and forgive her. When the countdown hit 0 James gave her a kiss while she still had her eyes closed praying. "Happy New Year, baby," He whispered. Billy watched James and Bridget from across the dance floor. Billy's date wrapped her arms around his neck and gave him a big kiss. She was a very beautiful woman, but so were all the women he would sleep with. It was now January and time for Bridget's monthly checkup. James came with her and wanted to be as supportive as any man in that situation could be. As they sat in the exam room Bridget couldn't help herself. They had to talk about this. They hadn't talked since the last doctor's appointment in December about the possibility those babies were Billy's. Staring at the checkered floor in the room she mustered out the words, "I am so sorry for this. I deserve to be punished for what I did, but not you." James looked at her for a little bit. She could barely see his brown eyes since he was wearing a baseball cap and staring into his lap. "You don't need to do that, Bridget. We will work this out. Even if these aren't my babies, we will work this out," He said. She hopped down off the table and gave him a big kiss on the lips. "I love you so much. Any other man would have walked away from me right now. You are still here. Thank you," She said to him. "No need to thank me, I love you and we are both responsible for this," He said with a little smile. Just then the doctor walked into the room. "Alright you two isn't that how you got in this situation in the first place?" He said with a chuckle. "Ok Bridget hop up here on the table so we can see how things are going. You feeling alright, any cramping?" Bridget shook her head no. "Ok well that is good especially if you are wanting to do this procedure. Any type of cramping we wouldn't want to risk it this early on in the pregnancy. Now if you are still on board with the procedure I do have to warn you that it is a fraternal pregnancy. Which means these babies were made from two different eggs. Which in turn means they could each have the same dad or both have different dads. I just wanted to throw that out there so there are no surprises," The doctor explained. Bridget felt even more apprehensive. "Does that happen that often?" She asked the doctor. "Not really, I haven't had anything like that happen in my career, but it is possible. So let us set up the procedure for early February. Would that work for you folks?" The doctor asked as James and Bridget both shook their heads in agreement. She felt extremely nervous and wanted it over with. She just knew these had to be James' babies. The month of January seemed to go by so slowly. The winter was rough. There was a lot of snow that month and February wasn't looking any better. Bridget told herself she was going to make that appointment even if she had to walk to it. But, there was also something else she knew she had to do. She needed to inform Billy that the test was going to be performed in February and that the results would be in within 72 hours. With the family being high publicity they told the doctor they wanted the results immediately. James already gave his DNA, now they needed Billy's. Bridget had been driving by the café for the past few days watching for Billy so she could tell him. Finally, she seen his jeep sitting at the café. She walked in with her head down and seen him standing at the counter grabbing his usual coffee. She walked up behind him and said, "Hi there, Billy." He turned around and looked at her for a moment and turned back to his coffee. "Hello, Bridget. What did I do to deserve this visit?" He asked stirring his coffee. "Um, the doctor is going to do a procedure here in two weeks and they need your DNA," She said watching him stir his coffee. Billy stopped stirring his coffee and asked, "My DNA?" "Yeah, we are going to find out for sure who the babies belong to," She said as he grabbed his coffee. "Not that I don't agree that that is a good idea, but your hubby just can't stand it can he? He has to know that you aren't carrying my bastard children," He said rudely to her. Bridget was disgusted by his attitude. "You really are a pig aren't you?" She asked him. "I am not a pig, no. But, I can tell you those babies are almost definitely not mine. I didn't even explode inside of you so that is nearly impossible. But, I will leave my DNA if it makes you happy," He said as he walked on out the door drinking his coffee and not looking back. The day of the procedure had finally arrived! Bridget was so nervous her hands were shaking. The doctor tried to assure her while James sat back in the chair with his knee jumping up and down. "Ok now Bridget, you will feel some pressure here. It shouldn't hurt too much, just a little pressure," The doctor said as he worked. After pulling the needle back out the doctor moved on to the next one and said, "Alright, good job that one is done and let me get the other syringe and do baby number two." Bridget squeezed her eyes shut while she felt the pressure push down into her belly. She felt like her belly was a balloon and the needle was getting ready to pop it. James watched the ultrasound screen like a hawk. "Alright, Bridget you are all done. Good job. We will rush these results for you and see you in here in a few days," The doctor said, as he started to stand up Bridget reached out her arm. "Oh, did Billy Hillenbrand leave his DNA?" She asked as the doctor turned around to answer her, "Yes he most certainly did. Now, you try to keep calm these next several days. You may have a little bit of cramping, but if it starts to feel intense you call the hospital immediately. No playing around, ok?" Bridget looked up at the doctor shaking her head yes. She looked over at James and let out a breath. "Are you ok? Do you feel alright?" James asked her. "Yeah, I am fine. I am just nervous. I couldn't wait for January to be over with so we could be at this moment. Now it is here I am scared," She said with a shaky voice. James stood up and walked over to her. "I told you, I love you and I am here for you no matter what. We are in this together," He kissed her hand as she laid there waiting for the doctor to give her the go ahead to leave. The last two days of waiting were horrible for James and Bridget. Billy didn't seem to care so much. Nobody noticed any difference in him. He was back to dating different women as usual. A few days after the test was performed they were called into the doctor's office at the hospital. James and Bridget sat directly in front of the doctor's desk waiting for him to come in with the results. Suddenly, they heard the door open. They both turned around to see Billy sit down by the door in the extra chair letting out a big breath as he got comfortable. "What the fuck are you doing here?" James asked in a nasty voice. Bridget just grabbed James' hand and said, "It is ok don't worry about it. He really should be here for the results." Just then the doctor walked in and asked, "Hello folks, how is everyone doing today?" Everyone seemed extremely fidgety and said they were fine. Laying the folder down in front of him on the desk he opened it to look it over for a minute or two. "What are you doing?" Bridget asked about ready to bounce off her chair. "I am sorry I need to read over this and make sure everything looks okay," He paused as he was reading through all the results. Billy looked around the room as if not to be too nervous or even excited. Billy had really shown up to get under James' skin, it was ridiculous to even think these babies could be his. "Everything looks to be completely fine with the babies. I don't see any abnormalities which is great!" The doctor said excitedly. "That is great news," Bridget said letting out a sigh of relief. "So can you tell us the rest, please?" She asked him nervously. "I am going to do that now, just be patient with me as I finish reading over the results," The doctor seemed to take hours reading. Even Billy seemed to be aggravated. They all sat in complete silence as they waited to hear the results.

CHAPTER 26

Finally, as he finished up his reading the doctor looked up at all three of them sitting on the edge of their seats. "So, here we go folks. I am glad to say that both babies have the same father," He said glancing up at Bridget's reaction. Bridget grabbed her chest and let out a breath thinking one of her prayers had been answered so far. The doctor went on to say, "Baby number one is a boy, and baby number two is a girl." Bridget couldn't help but smile getting tears in her eyes. Billy sat leaning forward with his hand resting under his chin as if to look bored. "It looks like both babies belong to one William Hillenbrand," The doctor said watching Bridget closely as she let out a low breathy, "No." James made a fist with his hand and squeezed his eyes shut as he bit on his bottom lip. Bridget reached over grabbing James' hand and said, "I am sorry." Billy sat in shock as the doctor walked past him patting his shoulder simply saying, "Congratulations." Billy all the sudden jumped up feeling pumped. Rushing out of the room he grabbed his cell phone excitedly and called Joey. "They are mine, did you hear me? They are mine can you fucking believe that!?" He yelled as he grabbed a few nurses and kissed them on the cheek. They giggled at his overexcitement. James jumped up out of his seat not being able to hold the rage in any longer. He rushed out of the room and punched Billy in the back of the head. "Woe, hey guys don't do this here," The doctor yelled as three more guys held James back. "What the hell, James? Can't handle the fact that you are a loser!?" Billy taunted him. Bridget slowly stood up from her chair so upset she was trembling all over. She made it to the door when all the sudden she collapsed on to the floor. Billy seen her fall and rushed to the room shouting, "Oh my god, where is the doctor?" James turned around trying to push the guys off of him as he shouted, "Let me go! That is my wife." James rushed over and said, "Billy get your hands off her!" He pushed Billy off to the side and rubbed her face calling out her name. The doctor ran over to check her vitals. Suddenly, Bridget came to and grabbed her belly in pain. "Oh god, it hurts. Oh no, don't let me lose my babies, god please!" She screamed as the nurses brought over a gurney. Billy and James both backed up in shock. Neither of them knew what to do. The doctor asked them to wait there while he put Bridget into a room to examine her. Billy and James sat far apart in the waiting room. Billy looked over at James and grumbled, "Why do you have to do this shit here? You will get your chance at me soon enough." James didn't say a word, he just looked at Billy like he wanted him to die. Finally, the doctor came back in. "The news isn't horrible. We did have to sedate her because she was hysterical. She should sleep through the night. Both babies seem to be doing fine at the moment. She did have a little spotting, but that is probably from the stress. You two need to try to be on your best behavior around her for the next couple of weeks. Amniocentesis is a very delicate procedure and add all this stress in with it, bad things can happen. So we are going to keep her overnight. Let her rest and we will check on the twins' heart rates tomorrow morning. If her cramping is gone and no bleeding we will send her home, okay guys?" The doctor asked as they both nodded their heads. "Can I see her?" James asked. "She is sleeping, but yes you can go in and check on her. It is room 322," The doctor replied. James thanked him as he hurried to the room. Billy jumped up and grabbed the doctor's arm, "Hey wait a second. Are my babies really going to be okay?" The doctor nodded and reminded him to not cause her any undue stress. Billy shook his head in a nod. "Got it. Is it alright if I spend the night in her room just to keep an eye on my babies?" Billy asked him. "I don't think that would be an issue, but I suggest you don't do it with her husband around," The doctor said as he walked off. James spent the rest of the afternoon watching over Bridget. He knew he had to get home to the kids so he kissed her on the cheek and left. He had been ignoring all the calls that were flooding his phone. Everyone already knew the sad news, but James didn't want to talk about it. He went to Emma's to pick up his kids and she was respectful enough to let the situation lie for now. She just cried and gave her big brother a huge hug. When James arrived home with the kids he waited until it was their bed time. He kissed them goodnight and called the hospital to see if Bridget was still alright. Then he sat down on his bed, all alone and cried hysterically. He felt defeated. Billy, meanwhile, went to his parent's house and was ambushed by his mom, Monica, Joey and Missy. They all hugged him and congratulated him. Then, Packard came walking up. "It is about time you made your old man a granddad, never expected it to be a Mackenvoy wife, but congrats all the same," He said as he squeezed Billy in his big arms. Walker and Jack just sat at the kitchen table rolling their eyes. Walker spoke up, "Yeah that is all we need another Billy running around. And a little girl, holy shit I can just see it now. You will have her in a chastity belt for the rest of her life." He finished laughing hardily. "Damn straight, nobody is going to get in my little girl's panties" Billy joked back. "That is a long way off, Billy! How do you feel?" Monica asked him. "I don't know yet, sis, it hasn't sunk in yet. I feel weird," He said smiling and shrugging his shoulders as everyone laughed. "It gets worse!" Joey yelled with Missy sitting on his lap. "Listen everybody I am going back to the hospital. I want to keep watch over my little treasures," Billy said as he went out the door. Monica watched him shut the door and then she shouted, "This is so exciting! I haven't seen this side of my little brother before. It is amazing. But, what does this mean with Bridget being a Mackenvoy?" She asked as she looked at Packard. "It means Victoria is going to be on a rampage and it means Colton is going to shit himself," Packard said with a laugh. Lisa rolled her eyes and said, "Do you have to always think this way? This is supposed to be a joyous time, not a time of war." Jack shouted, "Oh there will definitely be a war my dear, mark my word. They won't let this one go that is for sure." Billy arrived back at the hospital and told the nurses at the station he would be in the room all night. Those were his babies and he planned on being there for them. Quietly going into the room, he stared at Bridget's face in the dim light. He couldn't believe he was actually going to be a daddy. He wasn't even sure how he felt exactly about it yet. He watched her breath as she slept calmly. Scooting a chair over to her bedside, he rubbed her right hand. He noticed her left hand had an IV in it. He looked at her belly for a few seconds and then he started to touch it. Very slowly he rubbed her belly. To him this was all so foreign. He gently rubbed back and forth on her belly and all the sudden he felt a bump up against his palm. He jumped and raised his hand for second. Then he put his hand back on her belly, when he felt a moving sensation under his hand he got tears in his eyes and did a small giggle. He couldn't ever imagine that he would feel his children moving inside someone this way. He leaned in and kissed her belly and rested his cheek against it. Bridget took a deep breath and moved her head to where she was now facing him. He stood up with the tears still in his eyes, he moved over to be face to face with her. He watched her for a bit and then he gently kissed her on the lips. He rubbed noses with her gently as he stared at her face. She jumped and rubbed her face with her hand. Hoping not to wake her, he moved his chair back by the window and propped his feet up. Pulling his baseball cap down over his eyes he fell into a deep sleep. The next morning Bridget jerked awake early. It was still a little dark in her room, but she could see someone sitting over by the window. Squeezing her eyes open and shut a few times she called out, "James. James wake up." Billy heard her and woke up slowly raising the bill of his hat. Bridget squinted as she looked at him. She could tell it wasn't James since he had hair hanging over the tops of his ears being pushed down by his hat. "Billy?" She asked. "Yeah, it is me. I just thought I would stay to make sure everything would be ok." He said. "That wasn't necessary, I am in a hospital I think I am well taken care of." She grumpily said as she moved upright in the bed. "How are the babies?" She asked him. "I don't know there hasn't been any nurses in here yet today, but I will go get them," He said walking out of the room. The nurse came walking into the room smiling. Billy followed her, but quickly sat back down in his chair. "Good morning, Bridget. How are you feeling this morning? The nurse asked her. "I feel a little groggy and my mouth is really dry," Bridget answered her with a tired tone to her voice. "Do you have any cramping?" The asked touching her belly. Bridget answered the nurse by shaking her head no. "Well that is good. We will get the ultrasound machine in here and check on those little babies, get you some breakfast and hopefully let you go home today okay?" The nurse kindly asked. Bridget nodded looking down at her belly. When the nurse left the room Bridget looked over at Billy. She didn't know what to say. "I can't believe this happened. All over a stupid mistake," She said rubbing her face with both hands. Billy rolled his eyes. "I wouldn't say my babies are a mistake," He snapped back at her. "I didn't mean that, Billy. I meant us having sex. I would never say babies are a mistake," She argued as the nurse came back in the room with the ultrasound machine. "Let me take a look here," She said as she started to slide the wand all over Bridget's belly. Billy stood up and moved to where he could get a better view. Turning back to look at Billy the nurse asked, "Are you the father?" He shook his head yes and said, "This is my first time seeing my babies." The nurse smiled and said, "Oh well then we will just have to print you off a few pictures won't we? So here is baby number one, a little boy. He looks fine with a strong heartbeat and a kicker," The nurse giggled. Billy looked in awe. "Wow that is amazing. They don't look like babies though." He whispered. Bridget didn't look at the screen as much as she watched Billy's expressions. "And here is your little girl, and she also has a strong heartbeat. Everything looks great guys! I will print off a few of these photos for you and let your doctor know," The nurse said with a chipper voice. Billy took the pictures from her hand and sat back down in the chair ogling them. Laughing he said, "This is amazing. Look at that. Isn't that cool how they can take pictures through your belly like that?" He asked Bridget with a huge grin on his face. Bridget kind of smiled and shook her head yes. "God, I have to take these and show daddy," He stood up and started to leave the room. Bridget shouted as he got to the door, "Hey Billy!" He stopped and stepped back in. "Congratulations," She said with a smile. He smiled back and replied, "Thanks."

CHAPTER 27

News had spread like wildfire about the paternity of the twins. The intrusive reality cameras were beginning to take a toll on everyone. Colton and Packard realized it was too much and decided not to sign up for a new season of the show. Everyone was relieved. James was in terrible emotional pain when he was on his way to pick Bridget up from the hospital. He meant what he said about sticking by her no matter what. He loved her. It did not matter that she was carrying his biggest enemies' babies. When James made it to the hospital Bridget was trying to gulp down her breakfast. "Yummy, that looks tasty," James joked as he walked over to kiss Bridget. "It may look good..... hell it may even smell good but, it doesn't have a taste," She complained while James smiled at her. "How are you feeling this morning? Are the babies feeling okay?" He asked her with sad eyes. "Yes, they seem to be fine," Bridget answered slowly. "That is great, honey, I am glad," He said while Bridget smirked. He laughed, "No, I am. Just because they have Billy's blood in them doesn't make them bad. As long as they have you in them how could I not love them?" He asked her. He seemed completely genuine in his sincerity. Bridget was surprised. It made her feel very good, although she knew he was still hurting. He wanted those babies to be his so badly. But, James was a good man at heart. He would never treat anyone the way his mother tended to do. Billy was ecstatic at the news of being a father. He was quiet surprised at how he was feeling. He couldn't stop looking at those pictures of his angels. He showed everyone in his family with pride. He realized he hadn't asked Bridget an important question. He called up the hospital and asked for her room. As she and James discussed how their lives would go on no matter the recent development, the phone rang in her room. "Hello?" She answered. There was a long pause then she heard Billy's voice come over the line, "Hey, I am sorry to bother you, but I meant to ask you something." She sat waiting for him to finish. "Yes?" She said. "Should I come to your doctor appointments? You know, when you have them I can......" Bridget interrupted him quickly, "No I don't think that is necessary. Thanks for asking though." While she sheepishly glanced over at James. Billy held the phone for a few seconds. "Okay, that is no problem I just thought I would ask. So do you need a ride home?" James kept his eyes planted on Bridget the whole time curious as to who was calling. "No I have a ride, thanks anyway. I need to go," She said rushing him off the phone. "Alright, take care then," He said looking up at the sky shaking his head as she hung up the phone. Bridget didn't want to seem rude to Billy and she realized he was wanting to be a part of the process. But, she had her marriage to think about and she knew Billy would have plenty of time with the twins when they were born. James asked her as soon as she hung up who it was on the other line. She hesitated before telling him. He rolled his eyes and looked at the door. "Look, this is only for three more months and we won't have to deal with him anymore," She said. "Three more months? Try 18 years, honey. You are going to have to deal with him for 18 years," James said angrily. She stared down at the blanket laying across her belly. "Well, he is a part of the babies' lives. He doesn't have to be a part of mine. You are my husband and you are one of the most important things in my life," As she finished, James spoke up, "What are we going to tell Megan and Dylan? They are going to notice their brother and sister look a little different. And they are going to notice Billy Hillenbrand packing them around." Bridget thought for a few seconds. "Kids are resilient. If they grow up in the proper household then they will only love their siblings no matter who their daddy is," She said sadly. James stared at her like she was talking in a foreign language. For the next two months Bridget kept to herself. She didn't go many places and she rarely seen Billy. She wanted things to be comfortable for James. She knew she was asking a lot of him. Everyone in his family still treated her well. Nobody talked about what would happen once the babies were born. Mostly, it was to keep Bridget from becoming upset. The pregnancy was high risk so she had to be kept as calm as possible. But, she still couldn't figure out why Victoria hadn't paid her a visit yet. Her curiosity was soon to end. It was late April when Bridget was having a cup of green tea at the café. Bridget's stomach dropped when she seen Victoria coldly sit down right in front of her, "Hello dear." Her words being like ice. "Hello, Victoria. What can I do for you?" Bridget rudely asked. "I see my son has still stuck by you even after all of this," Victoria said raising her brow. Bridget nodded her head yes. The whole café watched waiting for something to happen. "My son can be blinded by what he thinks is love, but if you truly loved him you wouldn't be hurting him," Victoria sneered. Bridget looked up from her tea into Victoria's dark soulless eyes. Victoria gave a small huff sound and went on speaking, "I love my children more than you will ever know and I won't allow you to have these gross spawns while you still carry the Mackenvoy name. Not why you are married to my son." Bridget began to feel aggravated, "It is a little late for that my twins will be born here in the next month……" Victoria nastily interrupted, "Do not have them in this town. For god's sake don't have them in this state! Do you really think that I will just stand back and watch this happen? You are wrong you little tramp. I have watched the pain on my son's face for the past five months. Pain you caused, not me. You should be ashamed of yourself. I can make things so hard for you. If you don't let my son go to be happy with a good wife, I can make your life a living hell. You don't know the power I would have over Megan and Dylan." The whole time Bridget sat looking down, but when Victoria said those last words she immediately looked up at her evil face. "You would turn my own kids against me? You are a mother how could you do such a cruel thing?" Bridget asked her in disgust as Victoria smiled. "I am a mother. A mother who only thinks of her family. You are not family. I don't know what you are but, it isn't family. I will do what I have to do to protect my son. Didn't he ever warn you, my dear? Family is everything to us. You are insignificant." Bridget had tears flowing down cheeks as Victoria spoke. Victoria stood up as she finished up her tirade, "Leave my son with what dignity he has left. If you are a good woman you will do this." As Victoria walked away, Bridget felt a huge lump in her throat. Looking around, she noticed everyone staring. She quickly wiped her eyes and stood up to leave. On the ride home she rubbed her belly wondering how a woman could be so vicious to the core. Bridget had to pick Megan and Dylan up from Cindy's house. She was kind enough to watch the kids while Bridget had her checkup. When she arrived at Cindy's house she was crying hysterically. Cindy wasn't sure what was wrong so she turned cartoons on for the kids so she could talk to Bridget. She explained everything to Cindy. Neither really knew what to say. Cindy quickly grabbed her phone angrily. "What are you doing?" Bridget asked her. "I am calling James. That bitch has gone too far," Cindy shouted. Bridget reached out and grabbed the phone from Cindy's hand. "No wait." She whispered. "What do you mean wait?" Cindy asked confused. "She is right," Bridget softly said. Cindy sat with her mouth gaping open confused at her attitude. "What do you mean she is right?" Cindy asked as Bridget stood up rubbing her belly. "I have hurt James so badly. He deserves so much more. Victoria is right. I am insane if I would think I could raise these twins under the same roof with James. I know he would be good to them, but Billy isn't going to allow them to stay in his home. You know the Hillenbrands. They will cause all sorts of trouble with me and James. They will want to try to take my babies from me," Bridget said as she stared out the door. "Bridget, I don't think it will get that bad," Cindy said. Bridget turned around quickly and said, "What kind of planet have you been living on? You see how crazy these people are. I just want to raise my kids to love one another no matter what their last names are. That won't happen if I stay in this shitty town." Cindy started to cry. "I am so sorry I wish I could help you," She said hugging Bridget. That night, Bridget made up her mind. She would sit down and talk to James. She would end what had been the most wonderful love she had ever felt in her life. She tried not to be too upset. It was so hard not to be. She could feel the twins rolling around in her belly like they knew something was wrong. When James walked into the house he could see right away she had been crying. "Oh my god, what is wrong?" He asked coming up to hold her in his arms. She cried even harder and held onto him like her life depended on it. "I love you so much and I have caused you so much pain," She said trying to pull herself together. He didn't know where this was coming from. He held her tightly and told her he had hurt her as well. But, she knew it had to be over. She took a breath and said, "James, you don't understand. I can't let you live like this. I can't ask you to put up with Billy every day after these twins are born. I can't see the hurt on your face every time you look in my babies' faces." James shook his head crying with intense pain as he asked her, "Are you leaving me?" Bridget grabbed his face and kissed him deeply before she vowed, "I am not leaving you for good. I just think for a while I need to give you your space. You need to see what else is out there in life. We will be so much better parents to our kids if we just let it go now while it is still beautiful. Once I have these babies things will get complicated. And I am afraid we will both lose what we have with each other. And our kids will suffer for it. I just want these kids to love each other. And I want you to be happy. That is all I have ever wanted." Bridget cried so hard she was afraid he couldn't understand a word she was saying. "I don't want to lose what we have either, Bridget. There has got to be another way for us all to be together," He begged as she shook her head no. "There is no way and you know that. We have just messed things up so much. This is the best way for everyone," She said sadly. They spent one last night together as husband and wife. They made love and held each other the whole night. The pain of having to let each other go felt unbearable. Bridget never told James about the visit from Victoria. But, in a sick way she knew she was right. James needed to be happy and dealing with Billy every day would have been too hard for him. Bridget knew their relationship would crumble and she didn't want to bring the kids down with them. She also knew if she didn't do this Victoria could very well ruin her life even more. If that was possible. She already felt like she was doing the most painful thing she was ever going to do in her life. Bridget decided it was best if she moved to a town in Kentucky, about two hours away from Pleasantville. There was no prenuptial agreement, but Bridget didn't want half of what James had. She just wanted help in raising the kids, but James wouldn't hear of it. In the divorce agreement he was giving her a decent amount of money to live on and child support, to Victoria's dismay. Bridget knew it would be too hard to see James when she would bring the kids, so she had her sister, Sophia, move in with her and bring the kids to him for his visitation. She never told Billy where she was moving to either. She sent him a note letting him know he would get to see his kids the same way as James would. The first week of May Bridget went into early labor. She sent Sophia on the two hour trip to Billy's home to inform him that it was time. Pulling into the hospital with Sophia, he was so excited. He hadn't seen Bridget in months. In the hospital, she was still referred to as Mackenvoy. She did as Victoria requested and chose a hospital nowhere close to Pleasantville. Sophia asked Billy if he was ready to be a daddy as they sat in the waiting room. He shook his head nervously and said,

"I am not sure if I will know what to do." He stuttered out his words while Sophia giggled, "I think you will be fine. You will have your family to help you. She is going to breast feed so she will send plenty of milk when you have the kids." Billy looked at her quickly with a confused expression. "How the hell is she going to do that?" He asked. "With a breast pump silly," Sophia said with a smile. He just looked at her strangely as he asked, "What the hell is a breast pump?" She looked at him oddly for a second and before she had time to answer a nurse came down the hallway. "Hello, so are you the lucky daddy, Mr. Mackenvoy?" Billy stood up and spoke a little sarcastically, "My name isn't Mackenvoy. It's Billy Hillenbrand. Make sure that is on my babies' birth certificates please." The nurse looked back at him as she started to walk down the hall and said, "Okay sir, I am sorry I didn't know. So on to business, she has had a c-section before so we will do the same procedure this time. Especially, since she is having twins." Billy nervously shook his head in a manner to let her know he was listening. He put on the scrubs he was supposed to wear and walked into the operating room. The sterile smell was very strong. He looked over and seen Bridget already lying on the table. He walked over to her slowly, "Hey Lady, how are you?" He asked her. She turned her head to look at him. "Hi Billy........ I'm scared," She said with tears in her eyes. He reached over and grabbed her hand as he said, "You will be fine. You are strong remember? You kicked my ass at that contest. I knew you beat me all along." She giggled at him as the doctor spoke loudly when he walked up to the table, "Alright are we ready to have some babies?" Billy looked down at Bridget and asked her, "Are you ready?" She shook her head yes and squeezed his hand. "I am glad you are here," She whispered to him. Billy and Bridget just stared into one another's eyes. After only a few minutes the doctor said, "Baby number one is a boy." Just then Billy heard his son cry for the first time. He looked at Bridget with tears in his eyes. "That is my son," He whispered amazed. A few moments later the doctor said, "And here is baby number two which looks to be a girl." Then no cry. Billy looked at the doctor. "Why isn't she crying?!" He asked nervously. The doctor didn't say anything as he continued to work on Bridget, glancing occasionally at the nurses that walked away with the baby. After a few seconds, they heard their daughter finally take her first breath. Billy took a huge breath himself. He walked over to take a look at his new little miracles. They were beautiful. He asked the nurse, "Are they supposed to be that tiny?" She smiled and said, "Yes twins typically are smaller than average babies. Now if you go on out to the waiting room we will let you see your babies as soon as they are cleaned up." Billy walked out to the waiting room to see Sophia eagerly waiting. "Are they all okay?" She asked. He smiled with the biggest grin as he said, "Yes, they are both healthy and screaming their ass' off." Sophia laughed and gave Billy a big hug. "We will get to see them in a bit. I don't even know what she planned on naming them," Billy said looking down the hall. "Well, she is naming your son Tyler and your daughter Kimberly." Sophia started to explain as Billy looked at her. "Supposedly, she said you like guns so that is why she named her Kimberly. You know after the gun, sort of," Sophia said with a confused look on her face. Billy felt touched all the sudden. "She remembered I liked guns and named her Kimberly. I need to go see her," He said laughing. "Oh wait," Sophia said before Billy walked off. He looked at her curiously. "She doesn't want you to see her. She just wanted you to be here for the babies. Now she has had them, so there really is no reason to talk to her," Sophia said sadly. Billy felt a pain in his chest. He felt immediately hurt, why would she treat him this way? He had no idea he wouldn't be seeing the mother of his children for a long time. "Okay, fine! I am going to go see my babies then," He walked off shaking his head aggravated. When he went into the nursery and seen the twins names written on their name cards he smiled. It was an unreal foreign feeling to him, being a father. He never could have imagined he would ever have kids. He stared at the babies and was suddenly afraid to touch them. He grabbed his cell phone and took a few photos to send to his family.

He tried to decide which one of his babies to hold first, then he reached down to hold his son first. When he picked him up he thought he would drop him he was so small. He kissed his little dark blonde hair and cradled him feeling tears well up in his eyes. As he held Tyler, he looked down at his little girl. He laid Tyler down softly and picked Kimberly up. He felt his heart melt as he stared at his baby girl. He was afraid he was going to break her. She had as much dark blonde hair as her brother had. Billy began to cry softly as he whispered, "This is so incredible. Who would have known I could love two people so much I have just met." Sophia stood by the door watching Billy with his babies as she smiled. Bridget laid in the recovery room, crying and thinking of James. She missed him so much. She had to fight the urges to call him. How was she going to get through the next few years? She was hoping the pain would go away over time but, what if it never does? James believed she would come back to him after a few years. But, her intentions had all along been to never come back to him………. or would she? Would she return to this town that had caused her so much pain? As soon as all four of her kids were ready, she would get up the nerve to come back. She would return to Pleasantville with a vengeance. After all, she still had a score to settle with Victoria.

ABOUT THE AUTHOR

B. L Bryant is an American author who resides in Indiana with her family.
She enjoys writing books of many different genres as a hobby.
She has enjoyed writing since she was a child, but didn't have the courage
to publish her work until now! She wants her books to be a source of enjoyment
for readers and make them feel like they are a part of the book as well!
She loves living out in the countryside and spending time with her family.